#5

BASES LOADED

Scrappers

#5

BASES LOADED

Dean Hughes

Aladdin Paperbacks

First Aladdin Paperbacks edition June 1999

Aladdin Paperbacks
An imprint of Simon & Schuster
Children's Publishing Division
1230 Avenue of the Americas
New York, NY 10020

Also available in an Atheneum Books for Young Readers hardcover edition.

Designed by Ann Bobco

The text for this book was set in Caslon 540 Roman.

Printed and bound in the United States of America

10   9   8   7   6   5   4   3   2   1

The Library of Congress has cataloged the hardcover edition as follows:
Hughes, Dean, 1943–
Bases loaded / by Dean Hughes.—1st ed.
p.   cm.—(Scrappers #5)
Summary: Because Gloria chews out her team members whenever they mess up, she sets the tone for infighting which in turn causes the coach to quit and leaves the future of the team in question.
ISBN 0-689-81928-5 (hc).—ISBN 0-689-81938-2 (pbk)
[1. Baseball—Fiction. 2. Teamwork (Sports)—Fiction.] I. Title.
II. Series: Hughes, Dean, 1943-   Scrappers #5.
PZ7.H87312Bas   1999
[Fic]—dc21   98-48758

CHAPTER ONE

Gloria Gibbs stepped carefully through the broken glass and rusty metal toward her brother Dale, who was at the controls of a huge car-crushing machine. As she approached him, the machine screeched into action. She put her hands over her ears and shouted at Dale, but he couldn't hear her over the noise. Finally, she tapped him on the shoulder and yelled as loud as she could, "Dad said you have to take me to my baseball game!"

Dale didn't understand at first, so Gloria pointed to her baseball glove. He nodded and pointed to his watch. "In a minute," he mouthed.

Gloria had spent the day working in the office at her father's scrap metal yard, and now she was glad to get away from the place. She walked toward the gate, where Dale's truck was parked, and sat down on the big chrome front bumper. Then she looked off toward Mount Timpanogos, which towered over the west side of the valley. Even though it was July, the peak was covered with snow.

In a couple of minutes the sound of the crusher stopped, and Gloria saw Stan, her other brother, walking with Dale toward the truck. "Hey, get off my bumper, dirt ball," Dale yelled as he approached. "I don't want you to dent it."

Stan laughed as though Dale had just cracked a terrific joke. Gloria did get off the bumper, but she told Dale, "Don't call me dirt ball, hog face."

Dale snorted like a hog—on purpose—and then gave Gloria a little jab in the ribs.

Dale was eighteen, Stan sixteen, and part of their daily routine was giving their little sister a hard time. Most of the time it didn't really bother Gloria that much. She could hold her own with them.

"Why didn't you bring your bike with you, *brainless?*" Stan said. "Then we wouldn't have to stop and run you into town."

"Don't give me that," Gloria told him. "You guys are glad to take a break. You don't *both* need to go."

"Shut up or we'll make you ride in the back of the truck," Dale said. He was grinning, but he gave Gloria another poke.

Gloria squeezed into the pickup between her brothers, who hadn't bothered to take off their grimy coveralls. They worked for their dad in the salvage yard in the summer, and by afternoon they were always covered with oil and dust. Gloria tried to make herself narrow, so she wouldn't touch them, but it was no use—as the truck bounced over the potholes at the entrance to the yard, both shoulders of her uniform got smudged.

"So, Gloria, do you think the coach will let you play tonight?" Stan looked past Gloria and smiled at Dale. They both knew, of course, that she was the starting shortstop.

"I'll not only play; I'll make sure we win."

"Oooh. Big talk from a little ol' girl."

Dale slapped the steering wheel. "What? You mean to tell me dirt ball is a girl? I thought she was our pet bulldog."

"I could bite your leg off, that's for sure," Gloria mumbled.

The brothers liked that one. Dale gave her a friendly but solid elbow that knocked her against Stan, who knocked her back the other way again.

Fortunately for Gloria, her brothers changed the subject after that. As Dale drove through the tree-lined streets of Wasatch City, he and Stan talked about the upcoming rodeo. Gloria listened in silence. This was typical. Her brothers didn't pay much attention to her, but when they did, they usually only teased her or knocked her around. They didn't ever hurt her, but once in a while it would have been nice to be treated like a real person—not a dirt ball.

When Dale stopped at the park, Stan let Gloria out, but then he yelled, "Hey, sis, be careful! Don't trip on those water skis you've got for feet!"

Gloria didn't turn around—she didn't want Stan to see her smile. Her brothers always made fun of the size of her feet, but the crack about water skis was a new one. She'd have to come up with a good comeback. Maybe something about his stupid haircut.

Gloria walked over to a group of her team-mates who were already stretching out for the game. "Hey, Jeremy," she said.

Jeremy Lim was bent over, trying to touch his toes. "Hi," he said, without looking up.

"What's the big deal, touching the ground? You're built right next to it. You ought to stretch as high as you can and see if you can't grow a little."

"Lay off, Gloria," Tracy Matlock said.

Gloria was taken by surprise. Jeremy's face had turned red. Didn't he know she was just kid-ding? "What are you talking about?" she said. "Jeremy's glad he's a midget. He has the smallest strike zone in the league." She gave Jeremy a slap on the back to show him she was only jok-ing, but Jeremy walked away without saying a word.

As soon as Jeremy was far enough away not to hear, Trent Lubak said, "For crying out loud, Gloria, why did you say that?"

"Hey, he *is* little. I wasn't trying to put him down."

Gloria looked around when she heard the coach calling the kids to the dugout. After they all walked over, he read the starting lineup—

which didn't have any changes—then paused and looked around at the players. "Kids," he said, "we get a fresh start tonight. This is the first game of the second half of the season. If we can win the second half, we still have a shot at the championship."

"We can do it, too," Robbie Marquez said.

"I think that's right, Robbie," Coach Carlton said. "No one thought we had a chance when this team got patched together, but we've shown that we can win. Now we've got to keep supporting each other and playing together as a team."

The coach's eyes were focused squarely on Gloria as he finished his little speech, and she could see that a few of the other players were looking in her direction. She knew what that meant: Everyone was worried that she was going to slip up again and start yelling at her teammates.

When the umpire called for the first batter, Jeremy put on his batting helmet and headed to the plate. "Let's go, Jeremy!" the kids were all yelling. "Let's get it going." But Jeremy didn't look natural at the plate. He was standing up too straight, too stiff. He swung at the first pitch even though it was over his head. The ball looped toward left field, but Gary Gunnarson, the Whirlwinds' shortstop, jogged back a few steps and caught it for the first out.

Robbie came up next and hit a hard grounder straight at David Park, the second baseman. Park made a good stop and threw Robbie out at first.

Gloria was walking to the plate as Robbie loped back toward the dugout. "Am I the only one who can swing the stick around here?" she said.

Robbie sort of rolled his eyes, and maybe he smiled a little, but Gloria wondered why he didn't throw some insult back at her. That's what she expected.

Gloria took a couple of pitches for balls, and then she got one she liked. She smacked a hard line drive at Russ Jenson, the third baseman. She thought it was past him, but he dived to his right and stabbed the ball out of the air. When he hit the ground, he actually looked around for a moment before realizing that the ball was in his glove. Gloria stopped in her tracks and yelled, "You lucked out, Russ. I don't think you even saw that ball."

She laughed even though the Whirlwind players got all over her. Everyone in the league loved to chew on Gloria, but that didn't bother her. She figured most of them were just jealous. She was one of the best players in the league, and everyone knew it.

The Scrappers' infield took some warm-up throws while Adam Pfitzer got his arm loosened up. Then the infielders threw the ball around the horn. Wilson Love, the Scrappers' catcher, finally zipped the ball to Adam on the mound and yelled, "Let's not give 'em a thing!"

But Chuck Kenny, the Whirlwinds' leadoff batter, was always a tough out. He fouled a pitch off, took one, and then poked a little fly ball toward Trent in left field. Trent stood his ground for a moment before he realized the ball wasn't going to carry very far. He charged then, but he couldn't get to the ball in time. It fell in for a single.

"Come on, defense, we've got to be quicker than that!" Gloria shouted. She was careful not to sound angry or critical. But when she glanced toward second, Tracy was shaking her head.

"Don't start that, Gloria," she said.

Gloria couldn't believe it. She wasn't mad at Trent. Now that she had a reputation for getting mad and chewing people out, the players watched every word she said.

Adam missed outside with his first two pitches to Jenson. Gloria didn't say anything, but she chomped on her big wad of gum. She really didn't want to see this game get off to a bad start, and it was frustrating to watch Adam have trouble throwing strikes.

After the third ball, Wilson tossed the baseball back and yelled, "Just settle down, Adam." Adam nodded, but when he turned to step back to the rubber, he glanced at Gloria—as though he expected her to say something.

"Chuck it in there!" she yelled, and she meant to sound positive. She wasn't sure it came out that way. But she had tried to help him with his pitching. He ought to know she was on his side.

"Ball four!"

Gloria allowed herself a little kick in the dirt, but that was all.

Wilson ran the ball back to the mound. He spoke quietly with Adam. Gloria started to walk over, but when Wilson saw her coming he gave Adam a little slap on the chest with his glove and jogged back to the plate.

Adam did get the ball over the plate, and Gunnarson swung under the pitch and lifted a high fly to right. Thurlow Coates was there for the easy out.

"All right! That's better." Gloria slammed her hand into her glove a couple of times. "You can do it, Adam. Let's see you put some mustard on it now."

The next batter, a guy named Friedman, helped Adam a little by swinging at a couple of bad pitches. Then Adam did come in with some heat on a 2 and 2 count, and the guy went down swinging.

"That's it. That's it," Gloria was yelling, and she felt good about showing her support.

But the next batter was a huge kid named Morton. The Whirlwind players all called him "Moose." The guy wasn't very athletic, but he had tons of power. The outfielders moved back. With two outs, Gloria dropped back a little herself.

Adam threw a pretty good pitch, but Moose clubbed it hard to center field. Jeremy took off for the fence, his back to the infield. With his speed, Gloria thought he might get there in time. But the ball dropped just beyond his reach.

By the time Jeremy fielded the ball and spun around to make the throw, one run was scoring and the runner from first had already rounded third. Moose was heading for second. Tracy had run into shallow center to take the cutoff throw.

Jeremy threw a dart to Tracy. Gloria glanced toward home. There was no chance for Tracy to make a play there, but Moose was slow, and Gloria was ready at second. "Second base!" she shouted to Tracy.

Tracy spun and fired, and the throw was perfect. As Gloria reached for it, she could hear Moose thundering toward her. The ball whapped into her glove. At the same time, she braced for the collision.

Moose didn't slow at all, and he didn't slide. He tried to run her over. Gloria held her glove in place, made the tag, and then drove her shoulder into Moose.

The crash was terrific. Gloria didn't knock Moose back, but she didn't get run over either. They hit the ground, and Moose never reached the bag. The umpire bellowed, "Out!" and the inning was over.

Moose jumped up quickly. He gave Gloria one quick look, filled with respect, and then he trotted off toward his dugout. Someone yelled, "Hey, did that *girl* hurt you, Moose?"

Gloria got up slowly, but she knew she would be all right as soon as she caught her breath. She heard Coach Carlton yelling to her, "Nice play, Gloria. Way to stick in there!" She expected some teammates to congratulate her, but the infielders were already heading to the dugout.

Tracy did jog toward her and say, "Are you okay?"

Gloria tossed the ball to the umpire. "I'm fine."

The outfielders were coming by now. "Hey, good throw, Jeremy," Gloria said. "I thought for sure Tracy was going to have to chase that ball, but you were right on target."

Jeremy nodded, but he ran past Gloria without saying anything. Gloria looked at Tracy. "Hey, what's going on?" she asked. "Don't I at least get an 'attaboy' from someone around here?"

"You don't understand, do you?"

"What?"

"You can't put people down all the time, and then expect them to tell you how great you are."

"I told you; I was only kidding with Jeremy."

"What if he had made a bad throw? You'd be yelling at him right now."

"No way. I'm trying not to do that anymore."

"They know what you're thinking. It's all Adam can do to throw strikes with you over there kicking at the dirt."

"Criminy, Tracy, what does he expect? The guy's rotten."

"And he knows you think so."

Gloria had no answer for that. She had thought it was enough to keep her mouth shut. What was she supposed to do now? Change Adam into a decent pitcher by *thinking* in some new way?

This whole team was a bunch of sweethearts anyway. She had never yelled at any of the players unless they deserved it. They just couldn't stand to be told the truth. If Jeremy didn't like to be called little—when he *was*—that was his problem. The guy ought to hang out with Dale and Stan for a few days and find out what some real insults sounded like.

CHAPTER TWO

Back at the dugout, Gloria still expected a few of the players to tell her what a great play she had made at second. But no one said a word to her. She couldn't believe it.

Thurlow picked out a bat and walked to the plate. He was in one of his silent moods again today. Gloria decided she would be like him from now on. She would play hard, say nothing, and let all the other players make the noise.

She watched as Thurlow took his casual stance. But then he took a smooth cut at a pitch and drove the ball to right field. The ball looked for a moment like it might curve foul. Thurlow didn't slow down, however, and his instincts were right: the ball bounced inside the line, and by the time the right fielder got to it and tossed it toward the infield, Thurlow was slowing to a stop at second base.

Gloria clapped her hands, but she didn't say anything. Everyone else was cheering for Thurlow and for Wilson, who was stepping to the plate.

Wilson let a couple of close pitches go by for balls, and the players in the dugout shouted, "Good eye."

"I make a great play, and no one says jack to me," Gloria mumbled to herself. "Now Wilson's a hero for not swinging his bat." But she wasn't going to worry about it. She was going to make so many big plays today, no one could possibly ignore her.

Wilson connected on the next pitch and shot a hard grounder between short and third. Thurlow hustled over to third, but the left fielder charged the ball quickly, and the coach signaled for Thurlow to hold up. Now there were runners at first and third with no outs, and the Scrappers were really talking it up.

The crowd was getting into the game, too. Gloria could hear Wilson's mom shouting, "Way to go, Wil." Gloria glanced around to see whether her own parents had come. Her mother didn't like sports, and she almost never showed up at the games. Mr. Gibbs had come a lot at the beginning of the season, but lately he hadn't made it very often. He kept telling Gloria that he shouldn't have sponsored the team; the Scrappers were a bunch of losers. That's what Dale and Stan heard all the time, so they made fun of the team—without ever coming to a game.

Tracy was up. She had become a tough line-drive hitter—better all the time—and never an easy out. Bailey, the Whirlwinds' pitcher, knew that, but he got a fastball over the middle of the plate, and Tracy met it on the nose. She knocked a solid shot into center field.

Thurlow took off for home and crossed the plate standing up. Wilson ran hard and made it to third. Tracy bluffed toward second, but the center fielder made a good throw, so she trotted back to first.

When Thurlow stepped into the dugout, everyone slapped him on the back or told him, "Good hit." But he paid no attention. He walked to the bench and sat down. Gloria was amazed that the players treated him so nicely when he acted like he hated everyone. But that was fine. Gloria could play it that way, too.

Trent was up to bat. He was also hitting much better lately—not always getting on base, but swinging well and timing pitches.

Bailey was struggling. His first three pitches were all low, the last one almost in the dirt. He stepped off the mound and thought things over while the Whirlwind infielders shouted for him to get the next pitch over the plate. That's what he did, too, but Trent wasn't taking.

He took a smooth stride toward the pitcher, swung hard, and *blasted* the ball to left field.

Gloria jumped up and watched the ball sail toward the fence. It was hit well, but high, and she doubted it would carry long enough. The left fielder got to the fence, stood and waited, but he didn't jump. He looked up and watched the ball fly out of the park.

Trent had stopped near first base. When he saw the ball disappear, he began jumping up and down. Then he remembered to run, and he went into his home run trot, circling the bases.

"That's his first homer," Robbie was yelling.

And then to Trent, "You're a *slugger!* A power hitter."

The dugout emptied, and Gloria ran out to home plate with the rest of the players. She waited her turn and gave Trent a two-handed high five—like everyone else—but she didn't say anything.

What pleased her most was that the team was up 4 to 2 now, and the Whirlwind players were all looking like they had already lost the game. But the Whirlwinds' coach was walking to the mound, and Gloria saw that he was waving for Gunnarson to come over from his shortstop position and pitch.

Gloria walked back to the dugout, where the players were still celebrating. Everyone was telling Trent what a star he was.

"Hey, Trent," Adam said, "you da man now. We expect you to do that all the time."

"I got lucky," Trent said, but he was still smiling and wide-eyed, like a little kid at his first fireworks show.

"Did you see that stroke?" Wilson said. He tried to imitate Trent's smooth motion, but it got translated into Wilson's strange style of swinging, and that made everyone laugh again.

Gloria liked all this, and even though she had promised herself that she wouldn't say anything, she did want to congratulate Trent. She decided to do it quietly. She walked down to him, gave him a slug in the shoulder, and said, "I'm proud of you, Trent. I didn't think you could do it."

Trent looked up at her, and his smile disappeared. "I know you didn't," he said.

"No. I mean it. I mean . . . way to go."

But Ollie Allman said, "You never think anyone can do anything—except yourself."

Gloria had been trying to say something nice. But now she was furious. "Shut up, Ollie," she said. "There's not one thing in this world I can't do better than you."

The dugout was suddenly silent. Gloria looked up and down the bench. Already, she wished she could take the words back. But she knew it wouldn't do any good. She walked over and sat down next to Thurlow. Then she put her feet up on the wire fence and leaned back—the way he always did. She wasn't going to say another word to these kids, ever.

Gunnarson had warmed up now, and Adam

walked out to the batter's box.

Tracy moved over next to Gloria. The two sat together in silence for a time. They watched Adam take a bad swing at a bad pitch and then lay off a couple that were even worse.

Tracy finally said quietly, "Gloria, I warned you, didn't I?"

Just then Adam poked a grounder through the infield for a single, and a cheer went up. Tracy jumped up and yelled, "That's it, Adam!"

Gloria didn't move, didn't say anything. When Tracy sat down again, Gloria told her, "I was trying to give the guy a compliment. What's wrong with everyone around here?"

"Gloria, think about it. First, you blow up last week and yell at everyone, and the coach has to send you to the bench. And then—"

"Hey, that's not fair. Coach told me to cheer for the team, and that's what I did. I thought all that was behind us now."

They both watched as Ollie hit a high pop-up into shallow left field. The shortstop backed up and snagged it. There was finally one away.

Jeremy walked to the plate. Tracy yelled to him to keep the inning going, but then she turned to Gloria and said, "Okay, you tried to do the right thing last time, but then you show up today, and what's the first thing you do? You make fun of a guy just because he's small."

"What are you talking about? That's just the way I horse around. All he has to do is call me something back, or tell me to shut up."

"There are things you just don't say, Gloria. They hurt people's feelings. You never seem to understand that."

"Only if I mean them. Can't these guys tell when I'm joking?"

"No, Gloria, they can't. You say everything the same way—like you're mad all the time."

Gloria exhaled heavily. Why was everyone so darned sensitive?

Jeremy went after a pitch and hit it hard on the ground. Jeremy dug hard for first, but the shortstop made a good pickup and threw under-handed to Park, at second. He stepped on the bag, made the pivot, and shot the ball over to Kenny, at first.

Double play.

The Whirlwinds had seemed ready to go down for the count, and suddenly they were alive and well, only two runs down.

There was a murmur of grudging respect from the Scrappers as they grabbed their gloves and headed for the field. Tracy stood up and looked at Gloria, who was still sitting with her arms crossed. Finally, Gloria grabbed her glove and got up. "I wasn't picking on him," she said.

But Gloria wasn't nearly so angry as she sounded. The only thing she could think to do was to shut up again. *If I don't say anything, they can't accuse me of putting anybody down*, she thought.

She took her position at shortstop and watched Adam throw his warm-up pitches. He was throwing the ball all over the place. She had talked to the numskull about his motion, and he had shown some improvement, but now she didn't know what he was doing. *Come over the top, you idiot*, she said—but only in her mind. If she had told him that out loud, the world would have come sliding to a halt, no doubt. She had to play with guys who didn't use their heads, didn't do what they had been taught, didn't even *think*, for crying out loud. And if she even suggested they do things right, suddenly she was the jerk.

She chewed hard on her bubble gum and

suddenly got so tired of the stuff that she turned her head and spit it out on the ground. She almost hoped that Tracy would tell her not to do that. Right now she was about as mad at Tracy as she was at anyone, and she wouldn't mind telling her so.

Instead, she clamped her teeth together and watched as Adam prepared himself to make a mess of a game that had started out pretty well.

CHAPTER THREE

Gloria heard Adam grunt as he released his first pitch. He was really trying to gun it. But the ball seemed to stick in his fingers. It hit the grass about halfway to the plate, bounced once, lost its momentum, and rolled across the plate. Wilson scooped it up and tossed it back to Adam. "Forget that one," he called. "It just got away from you."

But Adam was beet red. He turned around and glanced toward Gloria, and she could tell that he wanted to crawl into a hole and hide. She noticed, too, that all the other infielders were looking at her, not at Adam, as if to warn her not to say anything. That ticked her off all over again. She never gave anyone a hard time about that kind of mistake. She just got mad when people didn't use their heads.

The Whirlwinds in the dugout were all laughing, and Chuck Kenny shouted, "Hey, Adam, if you're going to throw the ball, you have to let go of it."

Normally, Gloria would have told Chuck to shut his mouth, but she decided she wasn't going to do that either. No matter what she said, she seemed to create a problem for herself.

David Park was the batter. He took another pitch, and the count moved to 2 and 0. Then Adam got a ball over the plate, and Park popped it straight up.

Wilson waved Adam and Ollie off and made the easy grab for the first out.

Tyler Waddups, the center fielder, walked to the plate. He went after the first pitch and topped the ball. He sent a slow bouncer toward third. Robbie took a couple of steps forward and fielded the ball on a big hop. That would have been fine had the ball been hit harder, but now Robbie had little time. He threw hard, but Waddups beat the throw.

Gloria had run over to back up Robbie. It was all she could do not to tell him what he had done wrong.

But the coach said, "Robbie, you have to charge a grounder like that. Especially when the batter is that quick."

Robbie nodded. "I know," he said. "I don't know what I was thinking." He took his hat off and used his wristband to wipe the sweat off his forehead.

Gloria walked back to her position. She was proud of herself for keeping her mouth shut. Robbie could make all the bonehead plays he wanted to. It was the coach's job to straighten him out.

Raymond Wing, the left fielder, was up now. Adam seemed to be settling down a little. He got ahead, 1 and 2, and then threw a good fastball. Wing swung hard but hit a high pop-up into shallow left field.

Gloria backpedaled to get into position. She held her glove up to shade her eyes from the sun, but just when she picked out the ball, Trent called her off. "Mine! Mine!"

Gloria veered off and turned to see Trent squinting and trotting carefully under the ball. But then he seemed to lose sight of it. He opened his glove wide and turned his head. The ball hit the heel of his glove and glanced off.

As the ball landed in the grass, Gloria leaped after it. But Trent got to it first and picked it up. Waddups had run halfway to second and had been ready to retreat. Now he had to take off for second. Trent gunned a throw to Tracy.

Tracy was ready, and the throw was there in plenty of time for the force. But the throw was hard and a little low. Tracy reached down, seemed to catch the ball, but then let it drop from her glove.

Gloria couldn't believe it! The play should have been an easy out—twice. She had had the ball all the way, and Trent had called her off. And then Tracy had taken her eye off the ball— or something. Sometimes the girl played like a ditz.

Gloria walked back to her position. She looked down at the red dirt of the infield and took long, even breaths. But she wanted to scream. She couldn't stand all these kids who claimed *she* was the problem. Maybe she got on people sometimes, but she didn't mess up one-tenth as often as most of them did. And when she did mess up, she didn't care if someone told her about it. That only got her going—so she didn't make the same mistake twice.

"Sorry, Trace," Trent called from left field. "I messed that up big-time."

"Naw, my mistake," Tracy said, but when Gloria looked up, she saw that Tracy was looking at her, not at Trent. And then she looked away the instant Gloria looked at her.

Gloria got ready for the next batter: Bailey, who had stayed in the game as shortstop. She smacked her glove—maybe a little too hard. And maybe that was her way of telling Tracy what she thought of her letting the team down. But Tracy couldn't accuse her of saying anything.

Bailey swung on the first pitch and hit a high fly straight into center field. Jeremy hardly had to move to make the catch. It was a routine out, but under the circumstances it deserved some praise. Still, Gloria didn't say anything. If she did, someone would tell her that her "tone of voice" was wrong.

Chuck Kenny was up again. He got around on a pitch, and it shot down the left field line. Robbie jumped high, but he had no chance to get it, and now the bases were loaded.

Adam took off his hat and wiped the sweat from his forehead. Then he dried his hand on his shirt. Two outs, bases loaded, and Russ Jenson was up to bat. The way things were going, Gloria figured Jenson was going to belt a grand slam. She just didn't trust Adam's pitching.

Jenson took a couple of sweeping warm-up swings, then stepped into the box and set his feet.

Adam looked nervous. He obviously was worried about walking a run in. He nodded when he got the sign—fastball—but then took a long time checking all the runners before he finally aimed a pitch down the middle.

Jenson let loose with a mighty swing. The ball whizzed up the middle on a line. It shot into the gap between center and right. Gloria saw Tracy run to short center to take the relay. Two runs were going to score, but there might be a play at third.

Thurlow was closing in on the ball, about to cut it off, but Jeremy was running hard, too, getting there at about the same time. Suddenly, they both backed off to let the other guy take it. Then they both went after it again. Finally, Thurlow lunged forward and grabbed the ball, which was slowing to a stop just short of the fence. In one powerful motion, he spun around and heaved the ball at Tracy. But he had put too much energy into the throw, and it was heading over Tracy's head.

Robbie saw the problem, and he took off after the ball at the same time that Ollie did.

Gloria ran to cover the bag at third. Waddups had already scored, and Wing went flying by, heading for home. Kenny wasn't far behind.

Robbie shouldered Ollie out of the way and managed to knock the ball down. Then he grabbed it and spun around. Wilson was yelling, "Home! Home!"

But the only play was at third now. Jenson was trying for a triple.

Robbie fired the ball to the plate anyway, and Gloria almost went crazy. But when she looked toward home, she realized what had happened. Wing had stumbled and fallen on his face, and Kenny had had to stop so he wouldn't run past him.

Wing had apparently landed flat on his chest and knocked the wind out of himself. He was only now struggling to his feet. The Whirlwinds had two runners between third and home and another one thundering to third from second.

There was nowhere to go, and all Wilson had to do was trot up the line and put a tag on Wing, who was still in a daze from his fall.

The inning was over, and only one run had scored. The Scrappers were still ahead, 4 to 3. Gloria took a big breath of relief. She couldn't believe how lucky they had been.

What shocked her was to hear all her teammates cheering and celebrating like they had just done something right. She couldn't imagine a more messed up play. No one had done anything right. They had only been taken off the hook by Wing's swan dive onto the ground.

The whole inning had been a mess. Players had dropped balls, failed to call for flies, missed the cutoff. And the pitching had been rotten. Now the players were acting like a bunch of stars. Robbie was yelling, "Nice job, Wilson," and Ollie was slapping everyone on the back.

Gloria looked at the coach. "What are they so happy about?" she asked, and she hoped he was as disgusted as she was.

But he laughed and said, "Hey, sometimes it takes a little luck."

That was too much for Gloria. She had to take a walk up the left field line. She promised herself not to say one word when she went back to the dugout. But she was steaming, and she wondered whether she could control herself if someone started spouting off about how great the Scrappers were.

She decided she was going to have to wash her hands of this whole bunch. Her teammates didn't listen to her when she tried to help them, and if she tried to get their heads in the game, they thought she was being bossy. If they wanted to accept their lousy play as good enough, fine. But she would keep *showing* them how the game was supposed to be played.

As she walked into the dugout, she looked the players in the eye, one at a time. She showed them with her frown that she found no joy in getting out of an inning by accident. She was glad to see that her stares seemed to quiet everyone, too. She walked to the end of the bench and sat down, but she didn't lean back like Thurlow. She was going to keep her head in the game.

The next few innings were much like the first couple: the Scrappers hit fairly well, but they played poor defense. Only the Whirlwinds' worse play kept them from making a game of it. By the top of the sixth inning, the Scrappers were up 11 to 4, but errors had given the Scrappers a lot of their runs. They couldn't depend on their bats against the better teams.

Gloria hoped the team could get a good rally going, get three more runs and end the game on the ten-run rule, but she didn't see a lot of intensity in the players. Now that they had a good lead, she could see they were taking things easy. There was a lot of laughing and kidding around, and even though Gunnarson wasn't throwing all that well, Thurlow, Wilson, and Tracy went down in order.

Gloria ran out to the infield, and she told herself maybe it was good that the team hadn't gotten another three runs. They needed a couple of good defensive innings to get back to a better groove.

But as she looked around, she seemed to be

the only one who was concerned. Everyone was tossing the ball around slowly, making half-hearted catches, and talking to one another instead of talking it up. She wanted to shout to everyone to get with it, but that was the old Gloria who would have done that. She was keeping her mouth shut now.

CHAPTER FOUR

The Whirlwinds hadn't played well, but they weren't about to give up. The first batter let a couple of bad pitches go by, then hit a hard-shot grounder past Tracy for a single. Thurlow tossed the ball in to Tracy, who relayed it back to Adam.

Adam did show some effort with the next batter. He tried to put some more "umph" behind his throws. The trouble was, he was missing. He walked the batter on a 3 and 1 pitch that looked like a perfect strike to Gloria.

"Come on, ump," she yelled, but then she stopped herself.

"Come on, kids, let's talk it up out there," Coach Carlton yelled. "We can't let these guys get back in this game!"

At least he sounded concerned.

The players did start some chatter. Gloria even yelled, "All right. Take two if you can, but get the sure one." No one could misunderstand something like that.

Bailey, the ninth batter, was coming to the plate. The Scrappers still didn't have an out. They needed this one before the top of the order went to work. But the umpire called a couple of pretty good pitches balls, and suddenly Adam was only two pitches from filling the bases. The next one was coming down the middle, and everyone knew it, including the batter.

Bailey didn't have much power, but he took a fluid stroke and poked a grounder to the left side. Gloria broke to her right, stretched, and backhanded the ball. She thought she might have a chance for the double play. She stopped, set her feet, and took a quick look to second. But she decided in an instant that she better take the sure out at third.

She spun and tossed a quick little throw to Robbie. But he wasn't ready. He was at the bag, but he was looking toward second. He reacted quickly, got his glove up, but Gloria had thrown awfully hard, considering how close she was.

The ball bounced off Robbie's glove, then his chest, and dropped onto the grass. He dived after it, grabbed it, and tried to tag the runner, but he was too late.

"Come on, Robbie!" Gloria shouted. "Be alive. What were you thinking?"

Robbie jumped up. He looked angry. "You looked at second. I thought you were going that way."

"Didn't you hear what I just told everybody? Take two if you can, but get the sure one. I had to take a look, but—"

"Gloria, never mind," the coach said. He was walking toward her. He put his hand on her shoulder and said, quietly, "You had time to look back at Robbie and give him time to get set. You hurried your throw more than you needed to."

"No way, Coach. My throw was on the money. He was gawking off in space somewhere."

"Gloria. Come on."

Oh, brother. It was time for another speech. But Gloria wasn't going to hear it. She twisted away from him and walked back to her position.

The whole team was silent now. All the chatter had stopped.

Then Jeremy yelled, "Shake it off, Gloria. Don't worry about it. Let's get this next guy."

Gloria turned and looked at Jeremy. She felt like running out to center field and pounding on that little shrimp. Hadn't he seen the play? It was Robbie who had messed up. But she only gave Jeremy a long glare, and then she turned back to see whether Adam could throw a decent pitch.

"I'm surrounded by losers," she mumbled to herself.

As Chuck Kenny stepped to the plate, the Whirlwinds really started whooping it up in the dugout. It was time for Adam to reach back and find some reserve strength. Either that, or they ought to try someone else—like Thurlow. If the coach would give the guy a chance, he could be a great pitcher.

But Adam decided it was time to get cute. Instead of throwing his hard stuff, he tried a change-up. Chuck almost jumped out of his shoes, the pitch looked so big. He got around on it and *thrashed* it. It was a spear, and it was flashing past Robbie when he lunged to his left and got a glove on it. It glanced sideways off the tip of his glove, straight toward Gloria.

The carom caught Gloria off guard, but she was able to reach down and scoop up the ball. She was off balance, but she recovered and fired the ball to second base. Tracy was ready. The ball no sooner hit her glove than she spun and whipped it to first.

The play at first was close. Gloria actually thought the runner beat the ball, but the umpire jerked his arm in the air. "Yerout!"

The Whirlwinds couldn't believe it. Their coach ran across the diamond, straight at the umpire. He was screaming, "That boy wasn't out. What are you talking about?"

But the umpire walked away from him and didn't reply.

Gloria loved it. One run had scored, but the Scrappers still had a big lead, 11 to 5. She laughed and yelled, "Two down. Take the easy one."

But she saw Ollie hurry to the mound and begin talking to Adam. She wondered what that was about, so she trotted over. When she got there, Ollie said, "That guy was safe. I know he was. Do you think we should tell the umpire?"

Gloria stared at Ollie for several seconds before she finally said, "Are you brain-dead? Are you on life support? Do I see tubes running up your nose?"

Adam said, "Lay off, Gloria. He just didn't know what you're supposed to do."

"Umpires call the plays, you pea brain. He wouldn't change his call just because *you* think the guy was safe—no more than he did for the Whirlwinds' coach."

Ollie looked as though he had been hit in the head with a bat. He mumbled, "I just thought..." and then he turned and walked away.

"Is this a zoo?" Gloria asked. She looked around. "Who let all the cuckoo birds out to play?"

"Lay off," Adam said.

"Let's see you make me."

"Gloria!" The coach was jogging to the mound. "Calm down. What's the matter?"

"I've tried all day to keep my mouth shut, but I can't do it. These people don't even know the game. They have black holes where their brains are supposed to be."

Adam looked at the coach, who appeared

confused. "Ollie thought that guy was safe. He wondered if he should tell the umpire."

Ollie was walking back toward the mound by then. "That's all right," the coach told him. "We let the umpires make the calls."

Ollie nodded.

Gloria was still dumbfounded.

"Do you see why I can't keep my mouth shut?"

"No, Gloria, I don't," the coach said. "But I'll tell you this much. You're about to leave this game again, and this time, you can just keep walking. I've tried all summer to get you to stop yelling at people, and nothing works."

Gloria rolled her eyes, and then she took a long breath. She began counting to ten as she turned to walk away. But just at that moment, Adam said, "I'd kick her off the team, Coach. She thinks she knows everything. She gets everybody messed up."

That was more than Gloria could handle. She spun around and yelled, "Adam, if you could pitch—even just a little—I wouldn't have to yell at you."

"Shut up, Gloria," Adam said. "Or come over here and say that."

Gloria knew she couldn't let that go by. She ran straight at him. Adam stood his ground, seeming unsure what she had in mind. But Gloria never stopped. She drove her shoulder straight into Adam's gut.

Adam folded like a jackknife and went down hard.

Gloria jumped up and stood over him. "Get up and fight me," she said. "Come on. Let's go."

But Adam curled up on his side. He was holding his stomach and moaning.

Ollie stepped toward the mound. "Do you want a piece of me, too?" Gloria yelled. "Go ahead. Take the first swing."

Ollie was stunned. "Swing?" he said. "Are you crazy?" He knelt down next to Adam.

But Gloria realized too late that he was only checking on Adam. She slammed him in the side of the head with her glove. He fell over and then scrambled up to his feet. "What's wrong with you?" he said.

But now everyone was coming over. Tracy tried to grab Gloria, but Gloria spun away, only to be grabbed by Thurlow, who seemed to have appeared out of nowhere. "Let me go," she shouted, but he had his arms around her, from behind, and he was holding her tight.

By now the Whirlwinds had crowded around, too. And the umpires were there. Gloria was still fighting to get loose, and she saw everything in a blur.

"You're out of this game," the home plate umpire told Gloria.

Like that was big news.

And then Coach Carlton spoke in a calm voice. "This game is over," he said. "We forfeit."

"No, Coach," Wilson yelled. "We've got the game won."

"That doesn't matter one bit to me," Coach Carlton said.

"Just kick Gloria off the team," Adam said. He was getting up now.

"What team?" the coach said. "Without a coach, you don't have a team. And I'm not going to coach you kids anymore. So you better start looking for a new coach."

Suddenly, the focus changed. All the Scrappers moved toward Coach Carlton. Gloria felt

Thurlow's arms loosen, and she jerked away from him.

"Don't do this, Coach," Adam was pleading. "We want to play."

"No, you don't," the coach said. "You want to have fistfights. I know baseball, and this isn't it. I don't want anything more to do with this bunch."

And he headed for the parking lot.

Gloria was finally calming down, and she felt sick to her stomach. She had ruined everything, and she knew it. But she couldn't say that now. She had dropped her glove at some point. She found it on the ground, and she headed away. She wanted to go to some place where none of these people could ever look at her again.

As she walked off the field, she watched the coach get in his old pickup and drive away. By now the Whirlwinds were laughing and mocking, yelling insults at Gloria.

That was fine. She figured she had all that stuff coming. No one was as mad at her as she was at herself.

CHAPTER FIVE

Gloria hated practicing the piano, but her mom would never let her skip a day. She had to play for half an hour every morning before she was allowed to do anything else. But today was murder. It was the morning after the coach had quit the Scrappers, and all Gloria could think was that her life was ruined. Every player on the team would hate her forever. She knew the whole mess was her fault, and yet she couldn't think of one thing she could do about it. Her mom told her that playing the piano would calm her nerves, but it was having the opposite effect.

"Gloria," her mom called from the kitchen, and then she walked into the living room. "What are you trying to do? Take out your frustrations on Chopin? Lighten up a little."

Gloria spun around on the old-fashioned piano stool. "Mom, can't I just skip practice *one* day?"

"Why skip today? You have nothing else to do."

"I don't feel like playing."

Mrs. Gibbs sat down on the couch. "Would it do any good if I called your coach and talked to him?"

"No."

"Don't you think he would give you another chance?"

"Mom, he's given me about a hundred chances already."

"Honey, I guess I don't understand. What happens to get you so upset?" Mrs. Gibbs was a large woman, strongly built, but she wasn't much like her husband. She was quiet, and even though she could be funny sometimes, she wasn't much of a tease.

"I want to win. I want our team to be really good. I don't care if players try hard and make errors; it just drives me crazy when they do stupid things."

"Maybe they don't know the game as well as you do."

"They don't."

"Can't you teach them?"

"I try. And that's what gets everybody mad at me. They think I'm some kind of smart mouth."

Mrs. Gibbs smiled. "Tell me about your tone of voice. How do you *help* your friends?"

"Mom, that's part of the problem. A lot of times I just kid around, and those numb brains all think I'm giving them a hard time. I'd like to turn Stan and Dale—or Dad—loose on them. Alongside them, I'd look like a sweetheart."

"Oh, Gloria." Mrs. Gibbs shook her head. "I worry about you. Your dad and brothers are all soft as marshmallows inside, but no one would ever know it. You've picked up all this rough talk of theirs, I'm afraid."

"I'd rather be like that than be some kind of little wimp, like Jeremy, and get my feelings hurt just because someone said I was little."

"And who was that someone?"

Gloria looked away. "Me," she said.

"When I went to your game that one time, I heard kids on the other team calling you a big mouth. How did that make you feel?"

"It doesn't bother me. They can call me anything they want."

"Really?"

Gloria thought about that. Names like "big mouth" didn't bother her. She didn't even let it get to her when they said, "Not bad—for a girl." But some things really did sting. She hated it when guys made her feel ugly—not a real girl— just because she was strong and good at sports. One time a guy had told her, "You're built like a workhorse, Gloria—except a horse is better looking." She hadn't given him the pleasure of seeing her flinch. She had thrown insults back at him. But that night she had stood at her mirror and wondered whether she really was that ugly.

"Do you think Jeremy hates being little?" she asked her mother.

"I don't know, Gloria. You know him better than I do."

"Not really. He never says anything."

"Do you ever try to talk to him?"

Gloria didn't answer. But now she had something else to think about.

"Honey, just finish your piano practice. But lighten up, okay?"

Gloria did play softer after that, and when she went back to her room, she spent some time thinking about Jeremy—and about herself. It was about eleven o'clock when her mom yelled up the stairs, "Gloria, there's someone here to see you."

Gloria walked down the stairs. "Who is it?" she asked.

"He's a boy from your team. But I don't know what his name is."

Gloria wondered what this could be about. But she was unexpectedly hopeful. "Thanks, Mom," she said, heading for the front door. When she swung the screen door open and stepped outside, she couldn't have been more surprised. She had sort of expected Robbie, or maybe Wilson, but it was Thurlow, and that seemed impossible.

"Hi," she said, and then she waited to see what he would say.

Thurlow had sat down in an old wicker chair on the porch. He glanced up at her and then looked away. "Hi," he finally said.

She waited. When he said nothing more, she said, "So what's up?"

"Nothing."

Again she waited.

"I was just thinking," he said, "that we ought to talk to the coach and see if he won't change his mind."

If Thurlow had said, "I've got an alien living in my basement," she couldn't have been more stunned.

"Do you think he would?" she asked.

"Probably not."

"He won't."

"Okay." Thurlow got up. He took a step to go.

"Do you think there's any chance at all?" Gloria asked.

Thurlow stopped. "My mom kind of thinks he might."

"Did she send you over here?"

Thurlow looked away again. "Yeah. Sort of."

"Thurlow, you don't even care if we have a team or not."

He stuck his fingers into the front pockets of his jeans, and then he looked straight at her. "I'd kind of like to keep playing," he said.

"Really?"

"We're starting to get pretty good."

"So is your mom going to talk to the coach?"

"She wants you to come over, so we can talk

things out. I told her I'd play hard the rest of the season. And you're going to have to promise to stop yapping at everybody."

"The coach won't buy that. I've promised too many times before."

Thurlow nodded. And waited.

"Well, I'll at least come over to your house and talk with Wanda."

"Okay."

Gloria ran back into the house. She found her mom in the family room. She had finally gotten around to reading the morning paper. "Mom, Wanda Coates wants to talk to me. She's our assistant coach. I'm going over to her house, okay?"

"Is she going to take over the team?"

"No. I don't think so. But she thinks maybe we can talk Coach Carlton into coming back."

"Well, good. But, Gloria, listen to me." Mrs. Gibbs set the paper down on the couch next to her. "Everybody likes to be treated with respect. You keep saying that your teammates are all stupid. Nothing's going to change until you stop talking—and *thinking*—that way."

Gloria said, "Okay," but it was a lot to think about, and right now, she was mainly interested in getting the team going again. So she ran upstairs, pulled off the ratty old T-shirt she had been wearing, and threw on a newer one. And then she ran back to the front porch, where Thurlow was still waiting.

The two walked down the street together, neither one saying a word. Eventually Gloria said, "It's a nice day," just to break the silence.

"It's going to be hot," Thurlow said.

"Thurlow, I don't get it. How come you've been dogging it all summer, and now, all of a sudden, you want to play?"

Thurlow walked for quite some time before he answered. Finally, he said, "Me and my mom had a big talk last night. I told her she's trying to run my life too much. She said she'd back off."

"What brought all that on?"

"The biggest thing was watching you yesterday. You were acting like such a jerk, and all I could think was that I had been acting like a jerk, too—only in a different way."

Gloria waited. Was that the end?

"But the big thing is that I want to beat the Mustangs. I want to shut those guys up. You and I are probably the best players in this whole town. Robbie's pretty good, and some of the other players are coming around. I don't see why we can't win the championship."

"You're forgetting one thing, Thurlow."

"What's that?"

"You hate me."

Thurlow looked over at Gloria, and then he smiled. "You're a pain in the butt," he said, "but most of the stuff you say is right. You know a lot about baseball."

"You were ready to kill me that one time."

"I know. And if you start mouthing off that way again, I still might."

"So what makes you think I can stop?"

"I don't know if you can or not. I just hope you can. My mom thinks I've got a bad attitude, but if I do, yours is even worse."

"I just lose my temper. That's all."

"No. It's more than that. You see everyone's mistakes. But you don't admit it when you mess up yourself."

That one hit home. Gloria's first impulse was to tell Thurlow to shut his mouth. The guy admitted he'd been acting like a jerk all summer, and now he was telling her how to act? But there was something about his honesty that she had to respect.

She didn't think he was entirely right. If she made an error, she could admit it. But she also knew that she had made that quick, hard toss to Robbie without giving him time to get ready. The coach had been right about that. There had been other times when she had made mistakes like that—and not been able to admit to them.

When Thurlow and Gloria arrived at the Coateses' house, Wanda said, "Come on in, Gloria. I'm glad you came over." The house smelled good, like oatmeal cookies. "Sit down."

Gloria sat on a long couch that was covered with a blanket. Thurlow sat at the far end of the same couch, and Wanda sat in a chair across from them.

"Gloria, would you like to keep the team together—and keep playing?" Wanda asked.

"Yeah, I guess I would."

"My phone rang off the hook last night, kids and parents all calling to ask me if I would coach the team."

"Is that what you're going to do?"

"Not a chance. I don't know the game well

enough. And more than that, Coach Carlton was trying to say something to you kids, and I'm not going to get in the middle of that. The only thing I'm willing to do is talk to him and see how he's feeling about the whole situation—now that he's had a night to sleep on it."

"Yeah. That would be good."

"I just don't know whether I can change his mind. He's got to believe that you kids won't fight with each other."

"The rest of the team won't fight—if I don't get things started."

"Gloria, help me understand. What makes you yell and get mad all the time?"

"Usually I'm not as mad as everyone thinks. I just sound that way."

"It's more than that, Gloria. We know you talk tough. But you were really angry yesterday. Even when you weren't saying anything, we knew exactly what was going on in your head."

"I don't want to be mad. I don't know why I'm like that."

"What if I talked Chester into coming back, but the players kept making the same kind of mistakes? Won't you just lose your temper again?"

"I don't know."

"Well . . . I've got to know. Is there any reason why Chester should trust you?"

"Maybe not. But my mom told me some stuff, and so did Thurlow—on the way over here—and I'm trying to think it all through. Maybe that'll help. I know I want to try."

"All right then. I'll go see Chester. But I don't know what he'll say."

Gloria nodded. She hoped things would work out. But she was also scared. She didn't understand why she got so much angrier than other kids, and she wasn't at all sure she could change.

CHAPTER SIX

Gloria walked home, and about an hour later she got a call. It was Wanda, who had some hopeful news. Everyone was going to meet that night at her house. The coach wanted to talk to the players before he made his decision. Parents were invited, too.

But when Gloria got to Wanda's that night, she didn't feel a lot of positive vibrations. The parents chatted with one another, discussed "the problem" a little, but the kids hardly said anything. And they especially said nothing to her.

Gloria sat by her dad, who was hopping mad. On the way over in the car, he had told her, "I already put out hundreds of bucks for those uniforms. If this coach of yours wants to quit, maybe I'll take over. I probably know more about baseball anyway."

"No, you don't, Dad," Gloria told him, and then she added, "Dad, I'm the one who messed up. Don't go over there and start yelling at people."

Now, sitting at the meeting, she wondered whether he would listen to her advice. Everyone seemed to be staring at the two of them, like they were the enemy.

Behind her, Gloria heard someone's mother whisper, "Is that her? She doesn't look so mean to me." Gloria rolled her eyes. What did the woman think she was? Godzilla?

Gloria had purposely put on a clean Utah Jazz T-shirt and her good jeans—without any rips in the knees. She felt a little like a criminal who got all cleaned up when she had to appear in court.

Wanda was the one making most of the noise. She was talking to everyone, trying to make people comfortable. She had everyone sit outside in her backyard, where she had dragged out all her kitchen chairs along with some folding chairs. As more people arrived, the kids gave up the chairs and sat on the lawn in front of their parents.

It was a pretty July evening and still long before sunset, even though it was after eight o'clock. There had been a thunderstorm that afternoon, and that had cooled things off a little.

All this time Chester Carlton was standing by himself. He greeted a few people, but he wasn't giving anything away about how he was feeling.

Finally, Wanda got up and said, "Well, folks, it's been fun to get to know some of you a little better. I sure hope there's some way we can work it out so we still have a team."

That didn't sound good.

"I guess you know we had a bad situation develop at our last game."

Of course, everyone knew the story, but Gloria wondered exactly what the kids had told their parents.

"And it wasn't just the little fight we had. There have been bad feelings among the players all along. I was pleased this morning, however, when I talked to Gloria Gibbs." Wanda smiled. "After we talked, I felt like we at least ought to get together and see whether we can't work some things out. That's what this meeting is about. The coach has a few things he wants to say. And then we'll decide what to do." She waved for Coach Carlton to come up. "Chester, you go ahead and say what you need to say."

The coach walked to the front of the group. He had dressed up a little. He had on a Western shirt, tan, with fancy snaps. He had bushy eyebrows and deep wrinkles around his eyes, but otherwise he didn't look all that old to Gloria. He had a brittle voice, though—sort of scratchy—and he didn't waste words. He always got right to the point.

"I quit yesterday because I don't like the way these kids treat each other. But, of course, it's up to you if you want to find another coach and finish out the season."

He looked at the parents for a time, and then he focused on the players. "In my mind, there's nothing better in the world than to play the game of baseball and play it well. On a good team, everyone thinks the same. They all trust that everyone will do what they're supposed to do."

Gloria thought she understood that, but she had the feeling that the coach knew more about the game—and the feeling he was talking about—than anyone.

"When I hear teammates get down on each other, yell and fight and all that, then something goes out of me. I just figure it's not worth it. That's not what baseball is about, and I can't do it."

No one said a thing.

"I'll tell you this much," Mr. Carlton said. "I thought this was kind of a ragtag team when I first met all you kids. For a while, I doubted whether you would amount to much. But we have some natural hitters here. Some good arms. Good speed. We've got the makings of a fine team. If you all wanted to work together, and pull for each other, we could be better than the Mustangs—and they think they're the king of the hill. Every now and then we've gotten it together for a while, and when we did, we looked really good. If we could do that, regularly, we could beat anyone."

The funny thing was, Gloria felt the same way. She had seen the kids really play well at times—and use their heads.

"But anyway, Wanda said come back and let's give 'er another try. But I'm not sure I want to do that. You look like a bunch of tree stumps. I don't see any excitement in your eyes. I don't know that any of you care about baseball enough to give it a go. And you sure don't care enough about each other."

Gloria's heart sank. This was no bluff. The coach meant it, and someone was going to have to convince him to change his mind. Ollie raised his hand, and the coach nodded.

"Some of us talked it over, Coach. We think we could stop all the arguing and stuff like that."

"You do, huh? Well, I've given you plenty of chances this season, and no one seems to listen to a thing I say."

And then Adam spoke up. "Almost all the trouble came from one player," he said. "If that person didn't play for us, we might be all right."

Coach Carlton stuck his hands in his pants pockets. He stared down at the grass for quite some time. "Well . . . now I've made up my mind," he said. "I don't want to coach you kids." He waited and stared into Adam's eyes. "You still think the problem is to find someone to blame."

"Now wait just a minute," a woman said

from the back. Gloria turned around and saw that it was Tracy's mother. "The way I heard it, one player was clearly out of line. I think the blame *should* be placed where it belongs. If that person can't abide by the rules, that person shouldn't play. The rest can get along with each other just fine."

Coach Carlton gave Mrs. Matlock a long look, and then he said, "You don't understand, ma'am. When it comes to fighting, one person— as you call her—was better at it than the others. But I don't see any *real* support anywhere. I understand that it might take a while for a team to blend, but we've hardly made any progress at all. I see a little sign of it once in a while, but then we're right back where we were."

"Well, maybe you need to *teach* them the attitudes that you want from them."

"Ma'am, the trouble is everyone wants to be the star. No one understands about teamwork anymore. So my suggestion is that one of you parents be the coach, and teach these kids whatever it is you want them to do. I'll stay out of it." He looked down at the players and said, "I'm sorry, but I can't do this." And then he began to walk away.

But Gloria said, "Coach, I *am* most of the problem. If I stop yelling at the other players, maybe everyone else will do the same."

The coach turned back, but he laughed. "Gloria, you're missing the point. I'm not talking about keeping your mouth shut. You tried to do that, and all that did was make you kick the dirt and smack your glove and look daggers at people. Everyone out there knew that you were expecting them to mess up."

Gloria understood that. It was exactly what she had been thinking about all day.

"Do you understand that? I'm talking about *thinking* different—trying to help another player, trusting each other. I was on a team one time with a little second baseman who didn't have much going for him. He wasn't quick, wasn't blessed with much talent, but the kid gave everything he had to the game, and he lifted the whole team. That's the kind of thing I'm looking for. I see some spark of that kind in a few of you kids—but we need that kind of attitude in every single one of you, all the time."

"I want to try to do that," Gloria said.

"You've said some things like that before. What makes you think you can do it this time?"

"I don't know. I just want to try."

There was a long silence, and Gloria watched the coach. But then the worst thing possible happened. Her dad had been fidgeting and grunting, and he finally exploded. "Aw, come on," he said. "Don't put all the blame on my kid. That Coates kid has more ability than anyone in this valley, and he won't say boo to no one. He don't play hard either. He just gets by. And these two big pitchers are both about half nuts. One talks to himself, and the other one doesn't know what planet he's on. If you want to quit coaching, you go ahead and sit in your rocking chair. You're probably too old anyway. I'd be just—"

"Dad, stop it!" Gloria was humiliated. "I'm sorry, Coach," she said. "I don't feel that way."

The coach was shaking his head. "Well . . . I don't think this is going to work."

"Wait a sec," Thurlow said.

The coach looked down at him.

"Mr. Gibbs is right about me. I'm as much

the problem on the team as Gloria is."

"I lost my temper, too," Adam said. "I called Gloria out. So some of it's my fault. I shouldn't have put all the blame on her."

The coach was silent now. He seemed to be thinking things over.

It was Wanda who broke the silence. "Kids, how many of you think you need to adjust your own attitudes?"

Every hand went up.

"See that, Coach?" Wanda said. "I think they're starting to understand. Could we at least give it a try for one more game?"

"Well . . . I suppose so," the coach said. "But you have to understand. I'm not playing games with you. I really can't do this if it's going to go the same way all over again."

"How many kids are willing to support each other and not criticize and argue?" Wanda asked.

All the hands went up again.

"All right," Coach Carlton said. "I forfeited that game yesterday. So that gets us off to a bad start for the second half. And I would like to win the championship."

"We can still do it," Wanda said.

"But even more than win," Mr. Carlton said, "I'd like to see you kids find out what it feels like to play on a real team."

So the team was alive again. Wanda brought out some cold drinks and cookies. Oatmeal cookies. Gloria had to wonder how she had known to make them that morning before she had even talked to the coach.

On the way home, Gloria told her father, "Dad, you shouldn't have made that crack about the rocking chair."

"Why not? That man is older than the hills."

"You're going to be old someday. Do you want me to say things like that to you?"

"It wouldn't bother me."

But Gloria didn't think her dad would like to be talked to that way—no more than she wanted some kid calling her ugly. She kept thinking about the word her mom had used: *respect*.

CHAPTER SEVEN

The Scrappers took the field first. They tossed the ball around, and they chattered the whole time. But Gloria was nervous, and she could feel that everyone else was, too. Billy Mauer, the leadoff batter for the Mustangs, stood close to the batter's box and timed his practice swings to Ollie's warm-up throws. Mauer didn't look nervous at all. In fact, he looked as though he had no doubt in the world that the Mustangs would win the game.

All the Mustang players were cocky. But they weren't mouthing off much today. They were probably too sure of themselves to bother.

Just before the game was going to start, Wilson ran the ball out to Ollie and then waved all the infielders over to the mound. "We can beat these guys," he told the others. "Ollie's really popping his fastball. He's going to have a great day. What we've all got to do is pull for each other, no matter what happens." He glanced at Gloria. "If you start losing it for some reason, yell at *me*, okay? I can take it."

"Or me," Robbie said.

"Hey, you can take it out on me, too," Tracy said.

"Get out of here, you guys," Gloria said. "I'm not yelling at anyone."

"Yeah, but don't just shut up. Then everyone wonders what you're thinking," Adam said. "You get that look on your face like you want to rip somebody's arms and legs off."

Gloria laughed, but she knew it was true. "Okay, I'll call you guys idiots if I have to yell at someone."

"All right, let's get it done," Adam said.

And from the outfield, Gloria heard Thurlow yell, "Let's go. Let's rip these guys."

It was the first time all season he had done that, and Gloria felt the electricity run through the team. Suddenly everyone was shouting with some confidence. Gloria yelled to Jeremy, "We're going to get these guys today. Let's do it."

Ollie's first pitch made Gloria feel even better. He didn't spend a lot of time talking to himself. He hummed one down the barrel and caught Mauer off guard.

Mauer stepped out of the box, and *he* talked to himself a little and then stepped back in.

Bam! Ollie came with another fastball at the knees, and Mauer took strike two. He stepped out again, and he seemed mad at himself. Then Ollie bent a curve over the plate. Mauer took a wild cut at it, and missed.

Strike three. One away.

"You're on tonight," Gloria shouted at Ollie. The whole team was yelling. "Keep firing."

Eddie Donaldson, the Mustangs' center fielder, stepped to the plate. Ollie didn't waste a second. He gunned another fastball. Donaldson swung hard but hit the ball off the neck of the bat. The ball looped toward Gloria. She charged it, took it on one hop, and in one smooth motion, shot it to Adam at first base.

As Donaldson turned toward the dugout, he was shaking his hands from the sting of Ollie's fastball in on the fists. Gloria laughed. She could see all the Mustang players on their bench, not yelling that much, and all looking a little shocked. They had to wonder what was going on with the Scrappers.

Adam clapped his fist into his glove and yelled, "Two out. Let's put these guys away right now."

Gloria looked to the outfield and held up two fingers, like horns. "Two down," she was yelling, and she loved the feeling out there. Everyone was yelling back to her, and they were all cheering for Ollie.

Sheri Gibby, the Mustangs' tall left fielder, was up next. Ollie threw another strike, but she timed it and drove the ball deep into left center. Jeremy took off like a shot. He closed on the ball as he watched it over his left shoulder. Then, just when it seemed it would be over his head, he reached up and stabbed it.

The Scrappers all cheered, and Gloria ran toward Jeremy, not the dugout. "Way to go!" she was yelling.

Jeremy smiled as he trotted toward her. "I didn't think I was going to get to it," he said.

"Hey, you can motor. I wish I had your speed."

Jeremy nodded, and Gloria could see how pleased he looked. She thought about apologizing for what she had said to him about his size, but she was too embarrassed to do that. She figured he knew she was trying to make things right.

Back at the dugout, everyone was excited. "We're going to do it today," Gloria yelled. "Let's get some runners on. Then Thurlow can knock one over the mountain."

Thurlow grinned.

As it turned out, Salinas, the Mustangs' star pitcher, was not on the mound today. The Scrappers were all talking about having no problem with this new guy—a kid named Justin Lou. But he looked great in the first inning. He got behind 3 and 0 to Jeremy, but as Jeremy looked for ball four, Lou was able to work the count full. Then he threw a great change-up, and Jeremy swung early and missed.

Jeremy shook his head as he trotted back to the dugout. Robbie walked to the plate, and Gloria went out to the on-deck circle.

Lou didn't have a lot of speed, but he moved the ball around, and he changed speeds with more control than most guys. He worked the corners and got ahead of Robbie 1 and 2. But then Robbie timed a curveball and stroked it over second base for a single.

Gloria wanted to make something happen now. But she knew she had to be patient with this Lou guy. He wasn't going to groove a fastball. She was going to have to look for something good to hit. She laid off a fastball that looked outside to her, but the ump called it a strike.

"Come on, ump," she said, without looking at him.

"Don't start with me," the umpire said, and she realized that it was the same man who had called their last game. She knew she better watch her step.

She took another pitch, not that different from the first, and this time the ump called it a ball. She didn't comment.

Now she was expecting a curve. And she got it.

She waited on the ball, and then she triggered. She knocked a hard-shot grounder straight at the shortstop.

She took off fast and glanced to see the

shortstop make a good stop on the ball and toss it to second. She knew the Mustangs would go for two. She had to run hard to beat the throw.

Gloria strained, drove hard, stretched for the bag, and felt certain she had tagged the bag before she heard the pop of the glove. But just as she relaxed to run on through, she heard the umpire shout, "Out!"

She pulled up fast, spun around, and shouted, "No way. Are you—" But then she stopped herself. The umpire was giving her a cold stare, just waiting for her to say the wrong thing.

She ducked her head, shut her mouth, and jogged across the diamond. Tracy ran from the dugout and handed Gloria her glove. "You're *blind*. Do you know that, Tracy?" Gloria said.

The coach was not far off. He twisted to look at Gloria—probably to see what was going on. But Tracy was laughing. And Gloria began to smile. They ran onto the field together. "He did miss that call," Tracy said. "But good job, keeping your control."

Gloria liked that idea. But she was a little ticked at the same time. The umpire had blown the call, and that had kept Thurlow from coming up with a runner on base. The Scrappers might have been up 2 to 0 by now. But she couldn't think about that. She just had to throw some leather at these guys and keep them off the scoreboard.

Alan Pingree, the Mustangs' powerful first baseman, was coming up first. The Scrappers knew this guy could hit the ball a mile. "Play a little deeper," Gloria yelled to Trent.

He nodded and moved back a few steps.

Ollie missed outside with his first two pitches, and that worried Gloria. She didn't want him to lose his confidence and start aiming the ball. But Ollie didn't seem concerned. He looked smooth on his next delivery, and he got his fastball over the plate.

Pingree got around quickly on the ball and jerked it hard to the left side. Both Gloria and Robbie broke for the ball. Gloria saw the ball skip just past Robbie's glove, and she took one more step and dived. The ball was just out of her reach, however, and it shot into left field.

As Gloria clambered back to her feet, she saw that Trent was sprinting up to field the ball, but he had a long way to come. Pingree was already around first, heading toward second. A good throw would hold him at second, but there was no chance to throw him out. She ran into short left to take the relay throw.

But Trent seemed to get overanxious. He tried to bare-hand the ball on the run, and it slipped out of his hand. He had to put on the brakes and go back for it. By the time he got the ball, Pingree was heading for third. Trent came up firing, though, and threw a strike to Robbie.

Pingree went into his hook slide, and Robbie set up just right, straddling the base. The ball came in low and hard. Robbie picked it off on one hop and swung his glove in front of the bag. He brushed his glove over Pingree's leg, and from Gloria's angle, it looked like he had the out.

The umpire was running up the third base line from home. He swung his arms in a wide arc and shouted, "Safe! Safe!"

Gloria couldn't believe it. Couldn't these guys get anything right?

Gloria felt the flame in her cheeks, but she didn't say anything. She spun around and punched her hand into her glove, hard enough to bust that ump's jaw. And then she talked quietly to herself. "It was close. Really close. The umpire had a better angle than I did. Maybe he *was* safe."

It was something she had never done much of in her life: admit the possibility that she was wrong. But it helped. She felt herself calm a little. Still, something else was nagging at her. There was no reason for the play at all, no reason to have a guy on third. What had Trent been thinking out there? He didn't have to hurry that much. If he had fielded the ball cleanly, Pingree never would have made it to third.

She spun around and walked to Robbie, and she said, quietly, "You don't have a brain in your head, you know that?"

He looked surprised for a moment, but then he realized what she was doing. "Yeah, I know," he said.

But that was stupid. It didn't really help. She was still thinking that Trent had let the team down.

"Trent was too deep," Robbie said.

"What?"

"Trent was already playing Pingree pretty deep, and then you told him to go back more. When you did that, I thought it might be a mistake. Pingree hits more line drives than long shots."

"Why didn't you say something?"

Robbie shrugged.

"Hey, when I'm wrong, tell me." Gloria walked away, but she was amazed. Maybe Pingree was on third because of her mistake as much as Trent's. Robbie knew the game as well as she did, but she was the one who usually told people what to do. Maybe she was blaming other people way too often instead of looking to herself.

The next batter was a small, wiry kid named Stabler. All his teammates called him "Snake." He hit with a lot more power than he looked like he should. He stepped into the box, looked up the baseline at Pingree, and said, "Get ready. I'm bringing you home."

"Oooh," said Gloria, loud enough for Snake to hear. "You're scaring us."

She stepped up a little. She hoped the ball would come to her, and she would have a shot to throw out Pingree at the plate.

Snake slammed Ollie's first pitch deep into the outfield, over Thurlow's head. He ran all out but then let off and watched the ball drop beyond the fence for a home run.

The Scrappers were suddenly two runs down—and quiet. As Snake jogged around the bases with his elbows out, looking cocky, he asked Gloria, "Are you scared now?"

Gloria was about to let the kid have it. But she stopped herself. She had it coming. She had talked some smack with the kid, and he had shown what he could do. She told herself she was going to show these jerky Mustangs with her bat and her glove, not with her mouth.

"Never mind," she yelled to her teammates. "We're going to get these guys."

Gomer was up. He was a goofy kid, but he could play. He swung and missed a good fastball, and then he let an inside pitch go by. But on the next pitch he took a big swing and rolled a slow grounder past the mound. Gloria charged hard, snapped up the ball, and without raising up, fired to first. Gomer was out by a step.

Gloria took a look at the Mustangs' dugout.

She spotted Stabler, and she gave him a hard look, but she didn't say a word.

Now the Scrappers were yelling again. And Ollie was firing. He struck out the right fielder, and then got Lou on a ground ball to Adam, at first. The Scrappers were behind 2 to 0, but they weren't down.

As they headed for the dugout, Gloria slapped her hand against her glove. "Come on, we've got to hit now!" And she liked the way she felt. She was playing baseball—really playing—and that's what she loved most.

CHAPTER EIGHT

Thurlow was coming up first, and Gloria had the feeling something good was going to come of that. Coach Carlton yelled, "Don't swing for the fence, Thurlow. Get on base and get something started."

Thurlow nodded, adjusted his batting helmet, and stepped into the batter's box. But Lou didn't want to give him much to swing at. He kept the ball outside on the first pitch and then came inside with the second one.

Thurlow looked like a new guy out there. Only the toe of his front foot was on the ground. His bat was high, still as a stone, and his arms were swelling with power. His front shoulder was cocked, his eyes steady. He was like a spring, fully compressed, ready to uncoil.

Lou went back outside with the pitch, and

Thurlow couldn't resist. He took a fierce cut at the ball and drove it foul down the first base line.

"That should have been ball three, Thurlow," Coach Carlton yelled. "Don't get anxious. Make him come in with one."

Thurlow didn't show a reaction, but he obviously listened. The next pitch was off the plate again, and Thurlow let it go by.

And then, on a 3 and 1 count, Lou tried to come back inside. Thurlow stroked the ball so hard it whizzed past Billy Mauer at second base before he could move. The right fielder ran to his right and flagged the ball down.

Thurlow rounded first, shifted to another gear, and surprised everyone by taking off for second. The right fielder finally realized what was happening and chucked the ball as hard as he could. But the throw wasn't close. Thurlow didn't even have to slide.

So now the Scrappers had a runner in scoring position, with big Wilson coming up. The guy could tie the game in an instant, but he was just as likely to strike out.

"Knock it downtown," Adam was yelling.

But the coach had better advice. "Just meet the ball, Wilson. A hit's a run."

Wilson looked awkward, with his off-balance stance. But he took a smooth swing, and he bounced a grounder to the left side. Thurlow made a bluff toward third, and that seemed to distract Gomer. He looked Thurlow back, and then he threw a little late and too hard. The ball hit the dirt, and Pingree tried to dig it out, but it caromed off his glove.

Thurlow trotted over to third, and Wilson took a base on the overthrow. That brought Tracy up with the tying runs in scoring position.

Either Lou had lost his cool, or he didn't want first base open. He never threw Tracy a strike. He walked her on four pitches, and now the bases were loaded, with no outs, but the bottom of the order was coming up.

"Let's blow this game wide open," Gloria was shouting.

Trent looked nervous. Gloria could see how badly he wanted to come through.

Lou was obviously feeling the pressure to

throw strikes. His first pitch was over the plate without much on it, and Trent was ready. He yanked it toward Stabler at shortstop.

Stabler played it smart. He didn't try to throw out Thurlow at home. He flipped the ball to Mauer, at second, and Mauer made a good pivot. He gunned the ball to first for the double play.

So the Scrappers got a run, but now there were two outs. And then Adam tapped an easy grounder back to the mound. Lou grabbed it and threw Adam out. The inning was over, and the Mustangs still had the lead, 2 to 1.

Gloria grabbed her glove and yelled to the rest of the players, "All right. At least we got a run on the board. Let's stop 'em cold now."

All the kids were shouting the same kind of stuff. They ran out on the field and fired the ball around. Gloria loved the confidence she could feel.

It paid off, too. The catcher was up—a guy named Brandon Flowers. He wasn't much of a hitter, and he was slow, but he tagged a fastball pretty well. It looked like it would drop in front of Trent, but Trent got a good jump and charged hard. He reached down and caught the ball just before it hit the ground.

Trent stumbled as he caught the ball, but he threw himself forward, did a somersault, and came up with his glove held high in the air—just to make sure the umpires knew he had held on to the ball.

"All right!" Robbie shouted. "Way to hustle, Trent. Big play!"

Gloria agreed. It could have been a man on with the top of the order coming up. That was the kind of situation that could lead to trouble. She shouted to Trent, told him what a good play he'd made, and then she ran a little smack at Billy Mauer. She hadn't had so much fun in a long time.

Mauer looked eager. Maybe too eager. He swung at the first pitch, which was down low. He scooted a little roller toward Tracy. The only trouble was, it didn't have much on it, and it died in the grass, not far past the mound.

Tracy charged, and Ollie spun and went after it at the same time.

But Tracy took over. "I've got it," she yelled at Ollie, and she pounced on the ball. Then she flipped it underhand to Adam.

It was a bang-bang play, but the ump called Mauer out. Mauer fussed and complained about it, but all the noise didn't change a thing. He still had to head back to the bench and take his seat.

Gloria had to laugh when she thought about it. Once an umpire had made a call, she had never seen one say, "Oh, wait a minute. I think I got that wrong." So what was the use of arguing? She had looked just as stupid as Mauer, lots of times, and now she wondered why.

Donaldson was up now. He swung his bat a couple of times until Ollie came set, and then he waited, looking tense more than ready. Ollie threw a curve—something he rarely did on the first pitch to a batter—and Donaldson was clearly expecting a fastball. He swung too soon and got around on the ball, pulling it foul.

The umpire threw a new ball to Ollie, but Trent ran down the foul ball in the corner of the field. As Ollie waited, all the Scrappers were telling him to fire this next one past Donaldson.

Donaldson must have been sure he was getting some heat this time. But Ollie went with the curve again. Donaldson started to swing and tried to hold up, but the bat carried through, and the umpire called, "Steeerike *two!*"

Donaldson stepped out of the batter's box. He hit the ground with his bat, and then he took a wicked practice swing before he got back in the box. Gloria was sure the hard stuff was coming now, and she hoped that Donaldson wouldn't pound the ball over the fence.

Ollie wound up and kicked higher than usual, and with a full, powerful motion, he released a pitch that looked inside. Donaldson flinched and leaned away, but the ball broke over the plate. Ollie had thrown another curveball.

"Steeeeerrrrike *three!*" the umpire wailed.

And Donaldson tossed his bat—hard—toward the bat rack.

The Mustangs' coach chewed him out about that, and the Scrappers all laughed as they trotted back to the dugout.

"Three curveballs!" Gloria yelled to Ollie. "Great idea."

"It was Wilson's idea," Ollie said. "He just kept calling for them, and I figured it was the last thing Donaldson would expect."

Wilson was already at the dugout. He was pulling off his chest protector. He laughed, and he gave Ollie a high five. The two looked very pleased with themselves—and with each other.

The coach walked over, and he looked into the dugout. "Hey, is anyone around here having fun?" he called out.

"Yeah. But we need some runs," Tracy said.

"That's right. We do. But no matter what happens, this is how baseball is supposed to be. You kids are looking great out there."

"I'm going to get something started right now," Ollie said. He grabbed a bat and headed for the plate.

But talking was one thing, and doing was another. The Mustangs had a lot of confidence, too, and Lou was still humming the ball. Ollie got ahead in the count, 2 and 0, but then he chopped a ground ball toward second.

Mauer had to jump when the ball took a high hop, but he came down with it and snapped off a quick throw to Pingree, at first.

Ollie ran hard, but he couldn't beat the throw.

Jeremy, however, had better luck. Lou was keeping the ball down now, and Jeremy also hit the ball on the ground. But Snake knew he had some speed to deal with this time. He stepped forward but got the ball on an in-between hop. He knocked the ball down, scrambled after it, reached and missed it, and finally grabbed it too late. Then he made the mistake of throwing anyway. He winged the ball past Pingree, and Jeremy ended up at second.

This was the run the Scrappers needed, standing at second. And Robbie and Gloria were going to get the chance to bring it in.

Robbie dug in and got set. He waited on Lou, took a couple of pitches too low, and forced the guy to bring the next pitch up. Then he unloaded.

Robbie hit the ball square, socked a clothesline shot to left. But he hit it directly at Gibby, in left field. She took one step forward and stuck her glove out. The ball drove her glove back, and the pop of the leather echoed around the park.

But it was just an out.

Gloria had to do it herself now.

She felt good, confident, sure she would come through. She rolled her shoulders, pumped the bat back and forth a couple of times, and then she stepped to the plate.

The first pitch was low again, and she let it go by. But she didn't step out, didn't waste time. She stood her ground and stayed ready.

The next pitch was up a little more, but she let it go by, too.

The umpire called it a strike, and Gloria thought he was crazy, but she didn't say a word. She held her ground again.

Lou went after her knees one more time, and Gloria triggered. She met the ball flush, and it snapped off her bat. She watched it take off on a long arc, and she was pretty sure she had hit the ball out of the park.

She ran hard toward first, but she was watching the ball sail toward the center field fence. As she approached first base, she slowed and waited. The ball was coming down, and Donaldson was at the fence.

But the wind was blowing in, not all that hard, but steady. Donaldson actually had to come back in a couple of steps, and he made the catch.

The third inning was over, and the Scrappers were still down, 2 to 1. But Gloria had given it her best shot and come close to hitting the ball over the fence. She couldn't feel too bad about that.

And one thing she had to admit: These Mustangs were cocky, but they were also *good*.

CHAPTER NINE

For the next two innings the Mustangs didn't even get a man on base. Ollie was rocking them, throwing good stuff, changing speeds, and staying ahead in the count. When they did put the ball in play, the Scrappers' defense was great. In the fourth inning Jeremy made a long run toward left field and reached up for a great one-handed catch. Then in the fifth Adam broke to his right and stabbed a hard grounder, back-handed. Tracy covered the bag, and Adam turned and flipped the ball to her in plenty of time.

Those two plays kept the Mustangs from getting anything going. But the Scrappers didn't manage to score in the fourth or fifth themselves. The trouble was, they were hitting Lou, poking singles here and there, but no one could come up with the big hit that would bring in the tying run.

In the top of the sixth, the first batter for the Mustangs was a giant kid who had come in to substitute for Flowers. He was no hitter at all, but he swung at a pitch and rolled the ball onto the grass, not far in front of the plate.

Wilson jumped out and grabbed the ball, and he had all the time he needed to throw out the runner. But he didn't step inside the line enough, and when he made his throw, the ball hit the big guy's shoulder and bounced away.

Gloria's first reaction was anger. That was the kind of stupid play that could lose a close game like this. This sub had been a sure out, and Wilson had put him on base.

"That's all right, Wilson," everyone was yelling, but Gloria could feel her breath coming hard. She turned toward Robbie, and thought of spouting off to him—just to blow off some steam. But then she thought of what the coach had said. It wasn't just a matter of keeping her mouth shut. She had to *think* differently.

"I could have done the same thing," she whispered to herself. "Wilson would have thrown out most guys. But that runner was so big that Wilson couldn't make a normal throw."

She felt herself calm down. She thought of the possibilities. "Let's take two if we can," she yelled.

Mauer was coming up, and she needed to concentrate on him.

Ollie threw a stinger of a fastball, and Mauer swung way late. The ball bounced toward Tracy.

But it was Ollie who stuck his glove out and caught the ball. Gloria was already charging to second, to cover the bag. "Second!" she yelled.

Ollie turned and tossed the ball to her. The big runner was out by a mile. But Gloria had to stretch for the ball, and she was off balance. She might have had a chance to get Mauer, but not a good one. So she didn't rush a throw. She held on to the ball.

The important thing was, everyone had done what they were supposed to do in that situation, and the lead runner was gone.

But Mauer was fast, and he just might try a steal in this situation. Gloria walked to Ollie. "Let's watch Mauer. He might take off." Then she asked Tracy, "Who's covering second?"

"Donaldson usually pulls the ball," she said. "You better stay at home. I'll cover the bag."

Gloria would have liked covering the base. She suspected she was better at handling the throw from Wilson, on a steal. But she also knew Tracy was right about Donaldson. "Okay," she said. "Watch Mauer. We don't want him on second."

Ollie did a good job of keeping Mauer close. He tossed that way a couple of times.

So Mauer was still on first when Donaldson hammered a ground ball at Gloria.

Gloria scooped up the ball and shot it to Tracy. Tracy took the throw, dragged her foot across the bag, set her feet, and rifled the ball to first.

It was the smoothest double play the Scrappers had turned all year. And the top of the inning was over.

Coach Carlton was yelling, "That's how it's supposed to look out there."

He clapped hands with Gloria and then Tracy as they ran off the field. Gloria loved seeing him so pleased.

But now it was the bottom of the sixth, and

the Scrappers were still behind 2 to 1.

Gloria was leading off, and she knew she had to make something happen. She let a curve go by for a strike, and then she got a fastball. Instead of swinging, she squared off and laid down a bunt along the third base line.

Gloria was not as fast as Thurlow, but she got a good jump from the box, and she ran hard. Gomer charged the ball and picked it up all right, but he had been playing back. He tossed the ball to first, but the play wasn't close.

Gloria clapped her hands and walked back to the base. The Scrappers were all yelling, "Way to think, Gloria. That's using your head." She liked that.

Thurlow was up, and Gloria was looking for the long ball. All day she had been expecting him to tag one. But he mistimed a curveball and bounced a grounder to the right side of the infield. That moved Gloria over to second and into scoring position, but Mauer threw Thurlow out.

Wilson was up again with another chance to do some damage. He hadn't had a base hit all day—not even a very good swing—against those Lou curveballs. But this time Lou hung a curve out over the plate, and Wilson swung a little late but managed to punch the ball toward right field.

Gloria had to wait to see whether Pingree would catch the ball. Once the ball dropped over his outstretched glove, Gloria took off, but the ball didn't carry very far. Pingree ran after it, grabbed it, and turned around with his arm cocked and ready.

Gloria held up at third, Wilson at first. Pingree ran the ball back to the infield.

Now Gloria needed to get home. Chad Corrigan, who was hitting for Tracy and entering the game now, was coming up with only one out. If he could put the ball in play, Gloria was going to get to that plate, no matter what it took.

Chad had a tendency to swing at bad pitches, but he played it smart this time. He took two pitches low and got ahead in the count 2 and 0. But then he got a great pitch that he should have stroked somewhere. Instead, he swung under the ball and popped it up.

Billy Mauer trotted slowly toward the mound, got under the ball, and made the catch.

Now there were two outs, and Gloria was still on third. She couldn't stand to think that another inning could go by—with another scoring opportunity—and the Scrappers would fail again to get the score tied.

When Trent stepped in, she yelled to him, "Come on, Trent. You've got to come through for us." And she decided to do what she could do. On the first pitch she bluffed a move toward the plate, as though she were going to try to steal home.

Lou had to know that she wasn't likely to do it, but she wanted to keep his attention, throw him off any way she could.

The pitch was high again, and Trent let it go by. Maybe Lou was starting to wear down.

Gloria took a giant lead.

"Stay back a little," Coach Carlton told her. But Gloria was bobbing and faking, trying to distract Lou. Maybe she could get him to throw to third and toss the ball away.

Lou glanced at her several times, couldn't seem to keep his concentration, and finally stepped off the rubber.

Gloria walked back to the bag, but as Lou got ready and took his signal, she took her huge lead again.

Finally, he looked home and acted ready to throw. But he faked a pitching motion and strode toward third. Gomer had sneaked in behind Gloria, and Lou fired the ball to him.

Gloria had to scramble back and dive. But she reached out and got her hand on the bag just in time. Lou's throw had been a little high or she might have been picked off.

"Time-out!" Coach Carlton yelled, and then he walked over to Gloria. He put his arm around her shoulder and whispered, "Gloria, I can see what you're trying to do. But don't push it too far. If you get picked off, we're going to lose a great opportunity to get you home."

"A bad throw to third could bring me in, Coach."

"I know that. And keep bothering the pitcher. Just don't take such a big lead."

Gloria thought the coach was being way too conservative. Sometimes a runner had to take some chances and make things happen. But she said, "All right," and then she walked back to third base.

She did have Lou's attention, however; and even though she shortened her lead a little, she kept bouncing and yelling and bluffing moves to the plate.

Lou finally went home with the pitch, but it was outside. Ball two.

The Mustangs' coach was shouting, "Don't worry about the girl on third. She's not going anywhere. Just throw strikes."

Big Jack Gibbs had been pretty quiet today, but he bellowed, "Don't believe it, kid. Gloria's coming home. You better be ready."

Gloria laughed, and then she broke for the plate. She stopped as suddenly as she had begun, but Lou flinched, and then he stepped off the rubber again. He tried to act as though he weren't letting Gloria bother him, but clearly, she knew she was getting into his head.

The next two pitches flew high, and Trent walked.

Now the bases were loaded. But that wasn't all good. That put a force at every base, including home. And it brought Martin Epting up. He had gone into the game for Adam now. He would play right field, and Thurlow would move to first when the team went back on defense.

Martin was hitting a little better than he had

early in the season, but he was not someone Gloria ever really expected to come through. She felt like she had to get herself home if it was going to happen.

She went back to the superbig lead, even though Coach Carlton began to say, again, "Not that far, Gloria."

She was baiting Lou, forcing the issue. When he didn't throw her way, she took one more step. She was going to give the guy no choice.

Lou stared at her, and she faked a step, waited, and he stepped off the rubber again.

She walked back, glanced at the coach, but he shook his head. "Watch yourself," he said.

Gloria touched the bag, and then, as Lou stepped to the rubber, she walked toward home as though she were never going to stop. Lou was watching her, not the plate. Gloria told herself, if nothing else, she was going to confuse Lou so badly he would walk Martin, and that would get the game tied.

But Lou looked home, took his sign, nodded, and started his motion.

Then he made his pickoff move again.

Gloria saw she was dead and knew better

than to go back. She took off immediately for home. She didn't know how well Gomer would handle the ball, or how good his throw would be, but she figured she was going to have to run over the big catcher.

She watched the guy's eyes, saw him look for the ball and then reach for it. She was dead unless she took him out, so she bulled into him with her shoulder down.

But the catcher held his ground. She was the one who went flying. She landed outside the base line, on her side, and for a moment, she saw strange patterns buzzing through her head. But she was not so dazed that she couldn't hear the ump shout, "Out!"

She rolled onto her face. She didn't want to get up and look at anyone—especially Coach Carlton. She knew she had made a mess of things.

CHAPTER TEN

Gloria got up off the ground. She could hear all the Mustangs giving her a hard time. That bothered her some, but what she hated most was facing the coach. Still, she went straight to him. "Sorry," she said.

"That's all right. Just play defense. We have one more chance."

"I really am sorry."

"I told you, you had the right idea. But you have to listen to me, Gloria."

"I know."

At least he didn't seem all that mad at her. What she knew, though, was that all the players were hating her. She turned to go back to the dugout to get her glove, but Robbie was running toward her. He was carrying her glove.

She reached for it, but she didn't look him in the eye.

"Hey, you almost pulled it off," Robbie said.

"What?"

"You almost scored the run."

"Robbie, come on. I got picked off. I had the tying run in my pocket, and I let the guy throw me out."

"I know. But I could see what you were thinking. With Martin up there, it was worth a try. If Lou's throw had been bad—or Gomer's— we would have had a run. They made a good play, but you gave it your best shot."

"Robbie, if you had done something that stupid, I would be screaming at you right now."

Robbie shrugged. "Well, you shouldn't," he said. "You have to trust your teammates when they're trying to get a game won."

Gloria stared at him for a moment. He was right. But she really would have chewed someone out for doing the same thing. And that only would have made things worse.

Trust.

It had to go both ways. All ways.

She walked onto the infield. Thurlow tossed

her a ball on the ground for a warm-up. She fielded it and threw back to him. He was grinning at her. "I liked the way you went after that catcher," he hollered to her. "That took some guts."

She nodded, and suddenly her stupid play didn't seem so bad after all. What she knew was that she had to come through for this team.

When Ollie got ready to throw, she hunched over and watched close. She kept her weight on the balls of her feet. If the ball came her way, she wanted to be there to make the play.

Gibby didn't hit the ball to her, however. She poked a line drive into right. Martin ran hard, but he had to field the ball on one bounce. There was no question in Gloria's mind that Thurlow would have made the catch.

Sometimes Gloria wished the coach wouldn't worry so much about letting everyone play.

"Good job, Martin," the coach yelled. "Way to keep the ball in front of you."

Maybe. But if the guy had just—

She stopped herself. *I'm not as fast as Thurlow*, she thought. *Maybe I wouldn't have made that play either.*

Pingree was coming up. Clearly, Ollie didn't

want any more base runners—and maybe he was thinking about Martin, too. Pingree was left-handed, and if he pulled the ball, Martin might have to make the play.

Ollie tried to be a little *too* careful, however, and he got behind in the count. On a 3 and 1 pitch, Alan did get around on the ball, and he hammered it to right field, just as Gloria had feared.

Martin took off, running hard. He angled toward the right field line, but the ball got past him. Gloria had moved over to cover second, but now the play was going to be at third.

And then Martin slipped as he tried to stop. He landed flat on his rear end. He grabbed the ball, though, and he jumped up, set his feet— just the way the coach had taught him—and threw hard to Tracy in the cutoff position. Tracy caught the ball just as Wilson yelled, "Home!"

She spun, cocked, and released a bullet at home plate. Wilson was in the right position, blocking the plate. He took the ball on one hop, turned, and got the tag down. Sheri slid directly into the tag.

She was a dead duck.

But Wilson wasn't celebrating. He had spotted Pingree booking it for third. He shot the ball to Robbie, who put the tag on another sliding Mustang.

Double play!

Gloria leaped straight in the air. "Martin, way to throw!" she screamed. "Tracy, you've got a gun. What a relay!"

And then she yelled to Wilson and to Robbie. Everyone had played it smart and done exactly what they had been taught. Martin didn't have a lot of speed, not even a great arm, but once he got to the ball, he remembered to get his balance, and he knew where to throw the ball.

"You're great," she yelled. "You guys are really great. No kidding!" She was sort of amazed that she meant it, too.

Ollie was fired up now. He whiffed Stabler on three pitches, and the Scrappers headed for the dugout.

"Now we do it! Now we get some runs!" everyone was shouting.

The problem was, Martin was still up, since Gloria had gotten picked off during his time at bat. And following him was Ollie, and then Cindy Jones, whom the coach had just put in for Jeremy.

Gloria felt all her enthusiasm sink when she realized how little chance the team had of pulling off a seventh-inning comeback. These were three of the worst batters on the team.

But Martin looked determined at the plate: determined to walk. And maybe Lou was trying too hard to finish the Scrappers off. He missed the plate with his first three pitches. Martin finally took a 3 and 0 pitch for a strike, but then he laid off on a close one for ball four.

When Martin got to first, he took a lead and then started making a few bluff moves of his own. Gloria thought it was funny, since everyone knew he wouldn't run, but still, the guy was trying to make things happen.

Gloria hoped Ollie would hit behind the runner, but the coach had another thought. He touched his chest, his arm, his belt buckle, and then the bill of his cap. Whatever he touched after his belt buckle was the signal—and his hat meant "bunt."

Ollie squared off and then had to let a pitch

outside go by. Now everyone knew the strategy. The first and third basemen moved in. But on the next pitch, Ollie put down a perfect bunt. It was down the third base line, too far for the catcher to handle, but a long way for Gomer to come and get.

Gomer charged, and maybe he panicked a little. Ollie was not fast and shouldn't have been able to beat the throw, but Gomer hurried, and his throw pulled Pingree off the bag at first.

Safe!

"Great bunt!" Gloria was shouting. How many times had the coach worked on bunting technique? And now it had paid off. There were runners at first and second with no one out. Maybe Gloria was going to get her chance to make up for her mistake after all.

But it was too bad Cindy was in the lineup. She had never come through in a tight situation all year.

Cindy walked to the plate, but she didn't look confident or strong. She glanced back at the coach. Maybe he was thinking bunt again.

But the infield was in tight. Gloria watched the coach signal for her to hit away. Coach Carlton had worked a lot with her, and she was improving, but this was a tough time to find out how much she had learned.

The first pitch was outside, and Gloria didn't think Lou was nibbling at the corners. He was getting tired, losing his control.

The next pitch took off high. Cindy had to be thinking about a walk now.

But Lou came down the middle with a pitch, and Cindy reacted. She didn't swing hard. Her motion was fluid and easy. She met the ball with a solid crack, and it jumped off her bat.

The ball flew into left center. The left fielder and center fielder both chased after it, but it got between them and bounced all the way to the fence.

Martin had had to wait for a moment to see whether the ball would get through, but he was going hard now. He rolled around third and went on to score. Ollie was making motions like a stork on land and going as hard as he could. He followed Martin around third as the throw reached the relay man.

The coach was waving him home.

Ollie galloped toward the plate, and the

catcher got ready to block. But the throw made the catcher stretch, and Ollie dropped into a hook slide—just the way the players had all practiced.

The catcher swung his mitt at Ollie's leg, and for a moment, in all the dust, Gloria didn't know.

But then she heard the magic word. "Safe!"

It took about one more second for Gloria to realize what had happened. The game was over. The Scrappers had beaten the Mustangs.

The *Mustangs!*

Everyone on the bench poured out of the dugout. But when Gloria looked around, she wasn't sure which player to jump on, or which one to carry off the field. It had been a team effort. Everyone had made a big play or two, and all the players had used what the coach had taught them.

They all ran toward home plate, collected around Ollie, but then they ended up in a crowd, all milling around, slapping one another on the back, shouting their joy.

"We can go all the way now!" they kept telling one another.

When all the fun quieted, and the Scrappers

had slapped hands with the Mustangs, the coach called everyone over. "What a game!" he said, and he was grinning. "Kids, do you realize how well you played tonight? I hope you under-stand—we could have lost, and it still would have been a great game."

"We're going to beat *everybody* now," Wilson yelled.

"Well, I doubt it," the coach said. "Baseball is a funny game. A bounce of the ball, one bad pitch, a foul ball by a couple of inches—any little thing like that can turn a game around. But that's not what I'm talking about. I'm telling you that if you play the way you just did, you'll have a summer you'll never forget. You'll know what it means to be part of a real team."

Gloria smiled with understanding. She looked over at Thurlow, who gave her a little nod. "I still want to win the championship," he whispered.

And Gloria agreed.

TIPS FOR PLAYING SHORTSTOP

1. The shortstop is often the best all-around athlete on a baseball team. If you want the job, you need to be quick and well-coordinated, strong, and smart.

2. Set up right of second base and deeper than the other infielders. Learn to adjust your position according to the batter and the situation. Cheat in closer, for instance, with a runner on third. Shift left on a left-handed pull hitter. Your coach may want you to play at "double-play" depth—shallower and closer to second base—with a runner on first.

3. When a ground ball is hit toward you, get in front of it if you can. If it's hit slowly, charge the ball and try to take it on a good hop. If you stay back and wait, the ball may take a bounce that is hard to play, or you may field it too late to throw out the runner.

4. As you field the ball, stay low. Keep your glove close to the ground. Don't turn your head. Watch the ball all the way into your glove.

5. When you field a ball with runners on base, be certain to get at least one out. Don't go for a risky double play when the out at first looks certain. Put out the lead runner if you can, but once again, not when the play is uncertain.

6. When the ball is hit to the right side of the infield, cover second base. When the third baseman fields a bunt, cover third.

7. If the ball is hit to left or center field, position yourself to take the relay throw.

8. You often have a better angle to catch a pop fly hit behind the third baseman than the third

baseman or left fielder does. If you do, call for it and take it.

9. When a ground ball is hit between you and the third baseman, let the third baseman take it in most cases, but be sure to back him up. Of course, if you can get to it easily and the third baseman has to dive, call for it and take it.

10. If the ball is hit to the right side when a runner is on first, run to second and be ready for a possible double play. Stay behind the bag until you take the throw, then drag your right foot across the base as you throw to first.

11. When fielding a pickoff attempt or a throw from the catcher, straddle second base with your feet. Use both hands when applying the tag so the runner's slide doesn't jar the ball out of your glove. You are usually the one who covers second on a pickoff play. You can often sneak behind the runner without being spotted. But this is a play you have to practice. You and the pitcher must work together with precision.

SOME RULES FROM COACH CARLTON

HITTING:

Grip the bat with your hands touching and your knuckles lined up. Don't try to strangle the poor thing. As a young player, you may gain some bat control by "choking up" on the bat. That means moving your hands up the handle just a little—an inch or two away from the knob of the bat.

BASE RUNNING:

As you approach a base that you are planning to round, loop outside the base line so that you can make a smooth turn toward the next base.

BEING A TEAM PLAYER:

Support your teammates. You can help inexperienced players with some good tips, but don't offer those tips at a time when it will sound like a putdown. Never embarrass a fellow player in front of teammates or opposing players.

ON DECK: ADAM PFITZER, FIRST BASE/PITCHER.
DON'T MISS HIS STORY IN SCRAPPERS #6: *NO EASY OUT.*

Tuesday's game was under the lights. That meant that the game would begin in the light of day but end under the ballpark lights as the sun went behind Mount Timpanogos.

Adam warmed up with Wilson, and he felt good. He was in control of all his pitches. He just hoped he could win the game without embarrassing Stan.

At dinner, Adam's dad had brought up the whole situation again. "Uncle Richard told me what you did, Adam," Mr. Pfitzer had said. "It was good of you to help Stan out, and I guess your coach was great to him."

"Yeah," Adam said. "Coach showed him some things that ought to help him."

"See. That's exactly what I've been telling you. At this level, sports are not only about winning and losing. Stan just needs some help with his confidence. I'm glad you worked with him."

But warming up now, Adam was well aware that his teammates were going to be watching to see what he did when he pitched to Stan. And Adam told himself he would go after the guy like he was the Pit Bulls' best hitter—and Adam's greatest enemy. No one would have any doubt about his commitment to the team.

"Let's get this thing started," Adam finally said to Wilson, walking over to him.

"Yeah, you're ready. So am I," Wilson said.

* * *

The umpires were calling for the Scrappers to take the field. The coach called the kids together first and gave them the batting order—with no changes from the last couple of games. And then Adam walked out to the mound and took his final few warm-up pitches.

The ump called for the Pit Bulls' leadoff batter. Waxman. Adam remembered this guy. He was a decent hitter, but his real strength was his speed.

Adam definitely wanted to set the tone early—send the Pit Bulls the message that he was in charge of this game. He started with a good fastball down and in. Waxman took it, and it was close, but the umpire called it a strike.

Adam came with his curve. It was in tight and Waxman was leaning away as it broke over the plate. Strike two.

Now Waxman would be looking for a heater, so Wilson called for another curve. This one broke outside, but Waxman chased it and missed.

"Strike three—yer out!" barked the ump. Adam felt a thrill of satisfaction. Three pitches, one away, and his first K for the night. Adam loved pitching when he could control the ball that way.

"Atta way to do it," shouted Robbie.

"Keep 'em coming," Gloria yelled.

James Wayment came up next, looking very intense. Adam loved it when he watched the guy get gunned down by Gloria on an easy hopper.

Next came Lumps Lanman. He was a big, chunky guy, but he could really damage a baseball. Adam threw a fastball, a little outside, and hoped that Lanman would get too eager. But Lumps laid off the ball.

Wilson signaled for a change-up, and Adam liked the idea. He palmed the ball but threw with a full motion. The ball drifted toward the plate, and poor Lanman started his swing way too early. He did manage to make contact, but he pushed a grounder down the first base line. Ollie ran up and fielded it, and then he tagged Lanman.

It was a great start. Adam knew he had never pitched better. As he walked to the dugout, he heard the cheers, and his teammates slapped him on the back. What he liked best, though, was that he wasn't scared and worried. He felt focused on the game, and he wasn't tempted to drift off into his own fantasies.

Jeremy looked eager as he grabbed a bat. Adam suspected that he had something to prove—especially to Mr. Corrigan.

Wayment was pitching today, not Tony Gomez, the guy the Scrappers had faced twice before. The word was that Wayment was stronger than Tony, with a better fastball, but not much else. If the Scrappers could get timed in on his speed, the way they had with Jackson, they should be able to handle him.

Wayment showed Jeremy his fastball right off. And it definitely had some pop to it. It got past Jeremy before he could trigger.

Jeremy fouled a couple off, but then he swung and missed for strike three. Maybe Wayment wasn't going to be a soft touch after all.

Adam told Jeremy it was okay, but Jeremy looked disgusted with himself as he walked back to the dugout. Adam thought he saw him take a quick glance at Mr. Corrigan, who was sitting in his usual spot at the top of the bleachers. At least he wasn't yelling . . . yet.

Robbie was ready for Wayment's fastball. He went with an outside pitch and punched it over the second baseman's head for a single.

Gloria wasn't scared either. But she hit a line drive right at Dave Boone, the shortstop. She almost knocked him down with the shot, but he held on. Two away.

Thurlow hadn't hit a long shot for a while. Adam hoped he would do it now. But he hammered another one at Boone, this one a hard grounder. And Boone was up to it again. He took the ball on a flat hop, caught his balance, and flipped the ball to Stan, who made the putout at second.

Adam had been hoping for another laugher, like the game with the Stingrays. But no such luck. The Pit Bulls looked tough today.

All the same, Adam kept his mind on the business at hand. When he went back to the mound in the second inning, he got ahead in the count to Krieger, a lefty, and then struck him out on a curve that broke in on his hands.

Boone fouled off three in a row, but then he got around on the pitch and smacked it into the gap between short and third.

Gloria chased it and managed to knock the ball down, but she couldn't make a clean stop. Boone was on.

Tony Gomez came up next. He was playing first base today. He was not a slugger, but he got on base a lot by spraying little line drives around the field. He could be overpowered, though, so Adam stayed with his fastball and busted some unholy shots over the plate at the guy's knees. Gomez fouled a couple off, but he never put the ball in play. He finally struck out when—after all the hard stuff—Adam surprised him with change-up.

Two outs.

Adam loved the frustration he saw on Gomez's face when he slammed the ground with his bat and then marched back to the dugout.

Wilson trotted out to the mound. Adam didn't know why. Things were going well.

"Tony is so cocky. I love to put him away," Wilson said. "You're pitching great."

"Thanks." But Adam waited. What was this about?

"Are you ready to take on Stan now?"

Adam had kept his focus entirely on Gomez. He hadn't even noticed Stan in the on-deck circle. "Sure," he said. "Why wouldn't I be?"

"Let's get him. Let's strike him out."

"You don't need to psych me up to do that. That's exactly what I intend to do."

"All right. Great." Wilson ran back to he plate and got ready. He called for a fastball and set the target on the inside edge. Adam knew what that was about: blast one in close, and put a little fear in Stan.

Adam nodded, but then he took a quick

look at Stan. He looked scared already.

Adam kicked and fired hard, but he missed his target and got the ball out over the plate. Stan let it go by, though, and the umpire called it a strike.

Adam couldn't believe how lucky he had been. He had given Stan a good pitch to hit—way too good.

Wilson called for another fastball, and this time he set the target low. But Adam was pumped. He forced the pitch a little, and it came in higher than he intended. The pitch was belt high and down the middle again.

Stan took a good stride, on balance, and a level swing. But he fouled the ball into the dirt. Strike two.

Adam took the throw back from Wilson, then stepped to the back of the mound and looked out at the mountain. He knew he needed to settle down and control the ball. A lot of hitters would have blasted that last pitch.

But he wasn't going to feel sorry for Stan. One more good pitch, and he could put him away.

Wilson signaled for another fastball, but Adam wondered about that. It was time to cross Stan up, change speeds on him the way they had done with Lanman and Gomez. So he shook off the sign until he got the signal for a straight change. Then he cupped the ball in his palm and fired away.

The ball seemed to glide toward the plate in slow motion. It took forever to get there.

But Stan wasn't fooled. He seemed to know it was coming. He waited, waited, and then took that smooth stride the coach had taught him.

He drove the ball hard, straight up the middle.

It was a clean single. Jeremy charged the ball and forced Boone to stop at second, but Stan had met the challenge and won.

Adam felt strange. He wondered what his teammates were thinking. He hoped they knew he had been trying to throw Stan off—not giving him something he could hit. But he also wondered about his decision. Now he wished he'd stayed with his fastball.

When Sarah Pollick came up, Adam knew he had to put her away, and not let Stan's hit make a difference in the game. He threw her an inside fastball that moved her back a little, and then he bent a curve over the plate. She mistimed the pitch and hit a comeback hopper right to Adam. He ran halfway to first and then tossed the ball underhand to Ollie.

And that was it for the Pit Bulls' at bat.

But as Adam walked to the dugout, Coach Carlton stopped him. "Why did you go with a change-up, Adam?"

"Just to throw him off. We've done that a couple of times today, and it's worked."

"Sure. But that works best with a big swinger, who's starting to time you. When you've got a guy overpowered, it's best to keep firing at him."

"Yeah. I thought the same thing . . . afterward. It was a mistake."

"That's all it was, wasn't it?"

"Sure."

"All right. Good."

Adam walked on toward the bench. He took some more slaps on the back, but he also noticed some sideways glances, even some whispers. He thought he knew what some of the players were thinking.

But he hadn't given Stan a break. He knew that much for sure.

Finally, Robbie said, "Hey, I thought you guaranteed us that Stan wouldn't get a hit off you."

Adam looked Robbie in the eye, and he said, loud enough for everyone to hear, "I should have stayed with my fastball. I tried to get too tricky, and it backfired on me. But he won't get to me again. That's a promise."

He looked around and tried to read their faces, but no one wanted to make eye contact with him.